A BROTHER TO DRAGONS

A Brother to Dragons

L.F. CHIESA

To my brother Mitch,
Dragon-heart, gone too soon

PROLOGUE

"I have a son named Aedan Q'tar."
The soft light barely reached the bed where the woman lay, her thin body restless beneath a tattered, coarse blanket. The whisper of sound came intermittently, barely audible, the same words over and over.

"I have a son named Aedan Q'tar...." Thick auburn hair, now greying about the small, pinched face, lay matted damply against the pillow. Blue eyes bright with fever stared into the dim recesses of the room.

A shadow rose from among the shadows of the corner, a heavily robed figure which bent first to lay another stick of wood upon the fire, then again over the woman, soothing her brow with a freshly dampened cloth and drawing the blanket more closely about her.

She turned her head to fix those bright eyes upon the one who nursed her. "I have a son named Aedan Q'tar." The words carried a weight of import, filling the spare room, weaving a throbbing web of satisfaction and warmth about the frail woman in her bed until the one who watched over her felt it to have a palpable presence. The last echoes of her whisper came back oddly stronger from the corners of the room, as though reflected back from some unseen source of confirmation. Her wan, pale face relaxed at last into a smile. Her lids fluttered like moths about a flame until the burning blue eyes were hidden. A log burned through, fell in the grate. She would never open her eyes again.

Chapter 1

Like a mosaic raised against the sky and crumbling at the top, the Monastery of Jethlah shimmered its rainbow colors in the distance. Topping a broad plateau, it stood clearly between two mountains, immense and immeasurably ancient.

No vision. This is some truth I should know.

The thought came unbidden into Aedan's mind as he and his companions, Barak and Obal, approached the monastery. The silent monks in their indiscriminate brown robes moved like a colony of ants in slow motion. At the well, Jeshimon lifted a yoke until it sat snugly across his shoulders, not so much as glancing in the direction of the approaching riders. Jubal smiled serenely and made the sign of the deity as mounts were reined in, a cloud of fine dust settling over riders, horses, and monks as Aedan and Barak dismounted. The Plain of Esdraegon was arid and hot, and the two riders eyed the glistening water as Jeshimon approached. As Barak, the smaller, darker of the two, began to speak, Aedan, taller and younger, slowly crumpled, collapsing into a heap in the dust. Obal, the third rider, leapt down agilely despite his bulk and aided Jubal in lifting his fallen comrade as Jeshimon brought forth a dipper of water.

She laughed, running through heavy blooms and knee-high grass, her hair unbound and yellow as the butterfly flitting in a come-hither dance before her. Dressed in a loose smock, the girl caught up her skirts as she ran, legs and arms bare and pale. Bees droned across a blaze of sun and crimson flowers; soft laughter drifted like a warm breeze in her wake. Against that light, she seemed to disappear, only to reappear by a bush of veldt berries growing by a stream.

'A changeling—wish-born light as a butterfly.' The thought came as unbidden as the image so clear within his mind as sounds focused at last in Aedan's mind, but with the return of full consciousness, the dream slipped away.

A faint, somber chanting drifted into the cell where he lay, for as Aedan opened his eyes, he could see beyond his pallet to the spare lines of the small chamber, uncluttered by possessions. Restless, he stirred and made to draw back the blankets in an effort to rise. A shadow moved forward and resolved into a smiling monk who gently eased him down, bathed his forehead with a cool cloth, and supported his head while holding a cup of water for Aedan to sip. He lay back, every muscle aching with weariness and wondered at the bitter taste of the water.

The smiling monk replaced the cup, nodded towards his patient, and left the cell. Moments later the sound of boots striking a hard floor reached him. A monk, hard to tell if it was the same one, appeared in the doorway, this time with Obal towering behind him. He strode forward.

"Ho, your spirit waxes strong once more, my friend." The monk vanished from the door as Aedan tried to find his voice.

"Do not make too great an effort to speak, my young friend," Obal cautioned, lowering his booming tones, "for I will tell you what you wish to know." At a nod from Aedan, the big man settled himself on the floor beside the pallet.

"We are come to the Monastery of Jethlah, which has stood for time immemorial between the two mountains. The monks take a vow of silence as novitiates, and those serve you now. We are to be given water and such supplies as would be furnished any wayfarer in need." He raised a hand in protest and lowered his voice as Aedan cleared his throat.

"It would be better, High-born, if you did not speak. Should those who seek you come this way, the good brothers will not be able to point with surety at you, and thus, they will aid us without effort." Obal's smile was the grimace of a wolf. He whispered softly as Aedan's brown eyes began to close, "we leave at dusk, when the heat of the day has settled. Barak tends our mounts even now." He did not add that the coming of darkness would provide a welcome cover for their flight.

Birds swept by in untidy flocks across a white-yellow blaze of light that furred the edges of the trees to black. They had come upon the monastery from the northeast and were now heading southwest into the gentler foothills of the Naransai mountain range.

Seek the high waters where the blood flowers bloom.

Aedan stirred in the saddle, startled. He had closed his eyes for a mere moment and this thought had arisen from nowhere to whisper in his mind. Barak, he noticed, had taken the reins of his horse and was guiding it through a rocky defile. This illness, it seemed to come and go, but at the same time to grow worse because the intervals during which he was not aware of this world came with ever greater frequency. He shook his head, trying to clear it as the dark masses of rock through which they passed became indistinct.

Obal was singing. Fire-clouds clashed and danced above his throbbing head. *Cool water, clear, fast-moving and deep.* The image flickered in and out of his vision as he tried to focus on his surroundings. The fire popped and crackled, the haze retreated. Nauseous, Aedan lay and watched the shadows flickering on the cave ceiling before turning his head. Barak and Obal sat across from him, eating in companionable silence. As the nausea passed and awareness was still his, Aedan rose up on an elbow and stretched a shaky hand to the fire.

"Well, my friend," Barak's relieved smile widened as he jumped to his feet, bringing a mug of water and a bowl across to Aedan, "think you that this soup is tempting?" He guided Aedan's hand with care from bowl to mouth. Then, satisfied that the young man could take his fill,

Barak sat back on his heels and fed brittle sticks to the fire.

The sharp brown planes of his face became a part of the shadows playing over the walls, his black eyes staring without seeing at a stick in his hand. It snapped at the clatter of the bowl falling behind him. Barak turned to meet Aedan's wary eyes over the brim of the mug.

"This... water," Aedan hesitated, "what is it that makes it so bitter?" Obal, who was measuring out grain to the horses, answered with a short bark of laughter.

"Do you think that we would poison you?" he asked with mock reproach. As Aedan flushed, but made no reply, Barak spoke soothingly, as if to the child he had taught to ride.

"It is an herb the monks use to help one rest."

Aedan sighed, draining the bitter brew with a sheepish grimace. Brushing unruly brown waves from his eyes, he glanced from Barak to Obal and tried to think.

"How many days have we been riding since... since we left the holding?" he ended harshly.

"Nigh on three weeks, Aedan-lad, but try to rest now," Barak urged, "and we will talk as the sun rises on the morrow."

If you are able. The words, unspoken, seemed to hang in the air. His arms weak from the movement, Aedan pulled his blanket close. Even as he lay back, he felt consciousness receding.

The sharp click-click-click of hooves against stone sang in his head. His eyes opened on a barren slope, tried to focus, and could not. When next Aedan came to himself, his vision was focused on his hands. Gloved to protect them, a thin stout rope tied them to his pommel. His brain could not fathom the meaning of such a sight, and although he knew it should worry him, he could not hold a thought steady. Darkness hovered, swooped down upon him once again and into his mind another vision arose.

The eld.

The precise moment of awareness could not be pinpointed. There were voices speaking in a tongue he did not know and then there were no voices. Like the blinking of an eye, they were and they were not. There was darkness, followed by light. Gradually, his shifting moments of awareness allowed him to connect the moments of light to the voices. And with that momentary awareness, this point of focus held and now there were forms behind the voices. In spite of this, he sensed that he was both there among them and yet still *here*, elsewhere. He strained to see the faces beyond the voices and could not, the extra effort weakening his concentration. Just as suddenly, all light, all others, were gone.

Feeling the perspiration damp upon his temples, Aedan woke with a start. Late morning sunshine crept beneath a shaded window. Barak, Obal, and he had come down into Taavel, a small city nestled among the foothills of the lower Naransai Range, three days before. Putting up in a ramshackle inn on the outskirts of the mercantile quarter, Aedan had slept long and for once almost without the odd dreams which plagued him. The fever appeared to have left him, and though he was weak as a day-old calf, he considered what must be done.

Taavel had the calm, cheerful bustle of a matron—aging well and prosperous, fed by caravans crossing the Naransai and a satisfying local production of chilta-woven plaids and Lapsa gem-working. At its heart sat the solemn, unchanging Universitat—a renowned seat of learning for medicine, music, mathematics, and philosophy. Aedan's own tutors had come from this very school, and if he were blessed with the luck of his *m'airi*, old Dostven would have retired here long since.

Dostven might know ought of this strange and persistent fever, or.... Aedan hesitated, afraid to admit even to himself that these fevered images resulted not from illness. What if they rested within his own mind, what if madness itself threatened to engulf him? In the holding, whispers had now and then reached him—whispers and looks that followed him whenever his mother was spoken of—the hints that his mother had been a madwoman, sent away by his father to die.

Aedan thought of his father, the careful, quiet scholar Mikal. He had never discussed the woman who had been his wife and Aedan's mother with his son, but neither had he by the slightest word or expression led Aedan to believe that he was ashamed of her. It had been Barak, when Aedan was old enough and curious enough, to want to know more, who had advised him not to open old wounds and to leave his father be. They had loved deeply, Barak told him, and his mother had been a giving, loving, beautiful woman. She had been ill, could not live at the holding, and so she had left to seek a cure and had died so doing. But now, Aedan wondered. How much of what Barak had said was meant to protect a boy's memories? His illness, inherited from his mother? Was he too simply on the road to death?

By the light! He must know. Aedan struggled into his clothes and splashed tepid water from the jug by his bed on his face and hands. Obal and Barak, he knew, were putting in a quiet hour here and there about Taavel—in the market, in the open courts of tavernas and eateries, gathering the news since their last stop in a town. He would seek his old tutor now and be back again before the others returned.

Aedan felt the day crumble from him. Dostven's shaggy brows arched as the old man leaned forward, his voice quavering.

"You are reaching for your *m'airi*, my son. Not destiny—not what someone or something cold and impersonal has written upon your future. But, out of your past and your present, the future is being constantly created and recreated.

"The die is cast, the pattern broken—by everything you are, have ever been—by everyone you've ever met. Do you see? From the day of your conception, before you were born, you began to build the future which opens before you."

"But, Master Dostven, being ill was not, is not something I could choose or not choose to be," Aedan protested, his voice rising. "And what," he paused, collecting himself with an effort before blurting out his suspicions, "what if these dreams are not fever-borne, but a symptom of madness?"

For a long moment, Dostven said nothing. A single leaf fell in a drifting spiral from the spindly young maple that stood just beyond the open window of his rooms.

"You are not mad, my child." Dostven's pale silver eyes gleamed with a sudden shrewdness. "The fever, I think, is real. Yet, who is to say what effect it may have on the workings of the mind? To set it free," his voice dropped to a whisper, "to let it seek like minds." Aedan could hardly hear the old man. "You must stop running, Q'tar, and face your present. But be very, very careful that you do not let the Sindren Corps have the least suspicion, not a whisper, my child, not a word."

Too late for that warning, the grim thought intruded as Aedan marched across the university common towards the town, the hair still standing on the back of his neck. The Sindren Corps! Those black-hearted pariahs living on the edge of power—corpulent and gorged from a never-ending flow of victims! His hands clenched. To see them picking the leavings from another poor soul judged beyond the bounds they set for human behavior due their god—to have their ilk as advisors and overseers at every level of government from the Emperor's High Council to the village mayordomo, by the light, how it galled him! And yet, they took only what they were given in many cases.

As Zaavan had given his birthright—the holding—to them. How long ago now? After the unexpected death of his father. An accident, it was called—horse and rider carried away in the torrents of the lazy River Settern, swollen with late summer floodwaters. His father's body, broken and battered, had been recovered alive, although he never regained consciousness. Bitter memories flooded his mind. Barak and Obal, he saw now, had been prepared. Too sick to see it coming, without his father's protection, he had been powerless to stop Zaavan and fatal to have defied him at all, the fever evident—easy to give the traitor cause for taking total control. Yet, somewhere in this mess, something still puzzled him. Why had Zaavan not given him to the Sindren priests outright? Why had the traitor hesitated? Lucky for him that the man had, but Aedan had a queer feeling that a key piece of information was hidden from him, the key to it all.

The quiet of the green, with classes in session, was broken by the tolling of the mid-day bells. First a peal of notes, joyous and riotous as the sun-splayed oval across which he strode, then the sonorous tolling of the hour. One... two... three.... Aedan's world narrowed to the shadows about him and the waiting edge of sunlight. To walk into that sunlight, beyond the Universitat, was to die. The knowledge came swiftly, surely, born not of delirium and fear, but of absolute certainty. If the innkeeper or his lad—the mealymouthed youth who'd fetched them water—had spoken of his fever and his ranting, it would be more than enough to seal his death warrant.

To die! And yet, he strode forward. Four... five.... He could not turn aside. "Go forth and meet your present," Dostven had counseled. With a grim determination, Aedan reached for the dagger in his waistband. He would not step into the light and let death go unchallenged! The final peal of the bells began to ring as he stepped forward from the shadowed green to the busy street beyond.

Chapter 2

Jennet wept and Aedan could not understand her tears, or why the soft gulping sobs should not cease. A low chanting filled his ears.

'*It is not time! It is not time!*' Her frantic thoughts battered at him. '*In this moment*,' she thought wildly, '*we will be bound together in the flesh as we have been in spirit. Hold your palm to mine. See how the golden light diffuses, see how our hands meld into one another. The light intensifies.*'

'*What?*' Aedan's thoughts echoed his confusion. '*How slowly this aura dims! I see your hand, small, fine-boned, against my own sturdy brown fingers—my father's garnet gleaming in its bed of gold—until the light is gone and only two hands remain, yours trembling.*'

Moved by impulse, he grasped her hand and touched his lips to it. Sadness and anger vied for possession in her face. Dimly, he understood her anger. Forced to this bonding, having no choice at all, she damped down the fire in those eyes. The hand he held was cold, giving nothing. She would give nothing more. Now, he saw it clearly, before ever he had a chance to woo her, she closed herself into herself, secured and separated, with only the fever tying them together. How could he explain that he had not wished for those visions of her—or for this? She would not listen now if he tried to tell her. Her head bowed, the fall of golden hair hid her face from him.

'*Not yet! Not yet! It is not time!*' The cry from her heart nearly shattered her resolve, but she held to the remnants of self-control. Forlorn and tremulous, she would not cry aloud in this company.

The elders' voices faded, their chanting finished, the tie completed between their Jennet and the stranger she had drawn so precipitously into their midst.

Jennet sat the rugged, piebald pony, Bracken, quietly, her features as remote as the great, gray slash of stone that marked Wassen Tor to the west. Aedan sensed neither fear nor hostility in her still countenance. For a single, unguarded moment memory provided a vision of her laughing, joyous progress across a high meadow. The contrast with his present was too hurtful.

"Jennet?"

The faintest whisper of wind ruffled the hem of her hood. She did not stir, did not answer. Defeated, he mounted Dobbet, his own sturdy mountain pony, once again.

Camped for the night, their fire swelled, drinking up the darkness. High above, stars glittered in response. Aedan looked away, finally, from the gleaming night sky, pulled his blanket closer, lay down, and put his back to the night. They had, so far on this strange, cold trail into the mountains, found no need to keep watch through the dark hours. Whatever danger threatened in the world beyond, it touched them not upon this silent, relentless journey. At least now, sleep was deep and dreamless when it came, his fever gone. He closed his eyes.

The fire was dying when Aedan felt the soft tread past his face, the soft rustle of her cloak as she settled herself against him, felt the chill and the shivering she could not halt. He lifted the blanket and spread it over her, drawing her to his warmth within the circle of his arm. Every night the pattern was repeated. Try as she might to fight it, she could not warm herself, but would sit across from him until certain that sleep and warmth would not come, she crossed the fire to him.

Wary that first night, tense in every line of her. He had done then as he did now, had not touched her in any other manner, had not spoken to her. She was always up and gone before he awoke fully. Yet, sometimes before she fled, he felt as though they lay enmeshed bone to bone, sinew to sinew, her golden hair tumbling free and her arms locked about him as were his about her. Startled into hopeless longing by such thoughts, it was never so when he opened his eyes. She sat across from him again and he ached within himself.

As they traveled on into the mountains, Aedan came to believe that he was not dreaming, that as she slept, her guard was lowered and they were together—not body to body but soul to soul. At the slightest hint of consciousness, she closed herself off once more, completely, from him. Some part of her, some part unreachable by his mind, his touch, his words, trusted and loved wholeheartedly.

Now, drinking the last cold dregs of their morning brew, he thought it must be her heart that she locked away so tightly. And, anger rising, he thought she could keep it so, and then knew, futilely, that he could not deceive himself. True, he had not asked for this bonding, but now he could not imagine life without her.

Jennet huddled in her cloak and watched him silently, tormented by the very sight of him—her thoughts raw as a wound.

'I loved.' It was a bitter, soundless cry. *'I loved you from the first moment I touched you—the first moment I felt your presence against the wind, part of the dancing joy of sunlight dappling the high mountain stream. Like a thread run through a cloth, you wove yourself among my hours. I felt your spirit strong and vibrant within. I would always have you with me, always love you.*

'You—from some dark conflict, some lost battle in the valleys. If I never saw you, I would have loved you still. Yet, you came, tied to me, I saw at last, not because you loved, but because you were ill! A fever! A sickness led your soul to mine and all the glorious, shared moments were something you neither sought nor wished for. Turned to ash, dulled.

'A fever that burnt the two of us! How I pulled you across time and distance to me, out of danger. In the flesh, without even knowing that I did so—betrayed into this pain by my own inner self. There you lay and the reality was cold. Joined to you by the Elders in the flesh, as the fever bound us by spirit. Because they had not foreseen the power latent within me, because I might have been killed otherwise, because some

measure of pity moved them. I had no choice. No time for you to know me—no time for you to choose this bonding of your own free will.

'Now, your kindness sticks like needles pricking a sore. You will be all noble and honor and cherish that which you did not choose. But I will not yield to kindness. It will not be that easy for you. I will not play the game. Bound as we are, together until you have reached whatever it is that you seek—and safely. That is the duty laid upon me by the Elders.

'But, once your goal is reached, then will I turn my back upon you all—love and home alike—and seek my own far corner and some morsel of peace.'

It was a hard thought, that, harsh and cold as the stone that rose up about them. Deeper and deeper they penetrated into the mountains. Aedan wondered at the others—Obal and Barak. What had become of them in Taavel? What had they thought when he hadn't returned? He could only hope that they had eluded their pursuers. On his own, now, he'd find out what kind of man he was. His glance flicked briefly to Jennet. He did not understand how this bond had come into being between them, what it meant. That she had saved his life was clear. That she had not known that she did so was equally clear.

Now he measured the trail sketched before them, its far edge disappearing into the clouds. How high and for what? It seemed to him that they should be seeking a way out of these mountains, a way back down into the valleys.

Aedan sang the song of listening later as the wind keened clear and hollow around the notes. His world narrowed to the fashioning of those notes in his mind, of marshaling the words into the proper verses and to the feel of Jennet before him in the blinding fury of the snow storming down the pass. They rode together now for what little warmth it afforded them and for fear of losing one rider, one pony in the winter's tumult. Like a bright golden light, warm and serene, Jennet joined her voice to his, lifting the song above the weight of the clouds to the unseen gods.

For that must have been when the gods heard and raised their eyes to the plight of their supplicants. Out of the noise and swirling of wet, heavy flakes, a shape threw back the snow and waning light. Something square, substantial, rooted in the rock of the hillside loomed before them. A wayfarer's hut. Aedan nudged his weary pony towards it and slid off thigh-deep into the snow, then staggered to his feet and pushed a path to the hut. The heavy door swung open without a sound at his touch. Eager to get out of the cold, the ponies pushed past his shoulder into the shelter. Shutting the door behind them, the sudden quiet and freedom from the buffeting snow and cold overwhelmed him, and then Jennet swayed on the pony's back.

A cot stood near the massive stone mantel that crossed the entire south wall. A coarse, dry blanket lay folded at its foot, almost as though it had been put there in anticipation of their arrival. Lowering Jennet to the cot, Aedan unfastened her water-weighted cloak and drew the blanket over her. In what pallid light remained of day, he could see wood stacked high against the east wall. Kindling lay near to hand in a wooden box beside the fireplace. The ponies stood in the corner, nuzzled together, patiently bearing packs and saddles. First, a fire, then he would strip the animals and feed them. Jennet needed warmth and rest. Food could wait until she woke.

The fire burned steady and warm, hotter than he had intended. Snow melted and water gently bubbled in a pot to one side of the hearth. The ponies, dry and fed, settled in their corner. Another quick glance took in Jennet, still asleep on the cot. Her eyes opened, met his even as he watched, holding his own in that moment between sleep and full awareness. She neither spoke nor looked away.

After a long moment, it was he who turned back to the hiss of water hitting the fire and hastily yanked the pot away. The small room seemed filled with heat and light, dazzling his eyes as it reflected from the liquid before him. Aedan closed his eyes against it and found he could not rise, paralyzed before the fire, pot in hand.

Then he felt, from a long distance away, cool fingers loosening the pot from his grasp and then brushing his forehead. He tried, but could not open his eyes to follow her movements. Blind now, he felt her pull him to his feet and put her arm about him as she guided him stumbling to the cot. Her touch, her gentleness, enveloped him, and he tried to force his eyes to open once more. At last, he lay burning upon the cot. Molten heat and light staggered and flashed in fantastic shapes behind his closed eyes. The flames were consuming him, and neither the cot beneath him, nor even, now, the body to which he had once belonged, could hold him to reality. The fire ravaged his very consciousness. With all his strength, Aedan fought that final consumption, knowing and not knowing how he did so, that it would be the final loss.

Something small and cold pushed back the flames. He held his own. The coldness spread. He could feel again a touch upon his hand—disembodied perhaps, but still his own hand. Slowly, that chill touch spread, salving and spreading along his arm to his body. The dancing bursts of heat and light now raged behind the barrier of this cold—contained but not beaten. He strove again to open his eyes. Jennet sat beside him, both small hands clasped about his own.

He turned his head. Beyond her, against the flames, another figure loomed, hazy and quiet as a shadow. Through it, the very flames flickered and popped. Was it a shadow wrought of the fever which once more gripped him? As if in answer, Aedan watched in amazement as it turned its head to him and brilliant blue eyes blazed into his own. Somewhere, a soft voice was chanting against the night with a sweetness that tore at him, the last slow song of a soul departing this life and earth. That song filled his mind, the final remnants of the fire within him damped down to a dull glowing.

I have a son named Aedan Q'tar. Aedan jerked as if a hand had closed about his heart, then his eyes opened in astonishment. Jennet lay curled at his side, fast asleep. In the light which passed for morning, her face was wan and troubled, and obscurely, he was pleased—hoping those lines of worry were for him. And then, he thought with a wry grimace, just so much she would have done for one of the ponies. He resisted the urge to stroke the frown from her brow.

I have a son named Aedan Q'tar. Grief struck and spread as the memory of his feverish visions returned. His mother. Dying in this bare stone hut, yet joy filled her heart at the thought of her child. And that son! He could not comprehend the enormity of that dream and shut his eyes against the tears blurring his sight. Jennet stirred beside him. He wanted to hold her, to feel her softness solid against him, a buffer for the pain. But he could not take what she would not offer freely. With an effort, he willed his arms to stillness, and yet she did not rise, but burrowed beneath her cloak, nestling beside him until the light lengthened across the sill of the high windows and spilled upon the floor.

They breakfasted on the stew Jennet had put together from their stores the night before, the girl as stiff and mute as ever. He thanked her anyway for her care of him, but in the face of her impassive countenance, had no heart to tell her of his dreams. They packed the ponies once more, leaving the hut as they found it, sweeping out the ashes and the ponies' droppings as they went.

A frozen, glittering sunlight broke through the clouds beyond the highest peaks, cutting a narrow swathe across the far valleys like a single searching beam slicing the landscape. The thought stirred a certain uneasiness within him, but Jennet seemed to feel nothing, for she nudged Bracken into the lead. His footing nimble, Bracken stepped along the rock-strewn trail. On the sun came to meet them, slowly flooding the trail above them. Aedan hastened Dobbet closer to the other pony. Down, down the light flowed until Bracken raised one leg as if to step into the sun. Then pony and Jennet vanished. A horrific scream tore from Aedan's throat, as he and Dobbet in turn stepped to meet the light.

Aedan opened his eyes to see the back of Jennet, still seated on Bracken, descending around a switchback in the trail below him. Dazed and blinking, he took in the change in light, temperature, in sound, in smell, nudging his pony to a faster gait. Wherever Jennet led, he would follow. It was warmer here, the slopes covered with sprawling bushes that caught at their clothing as they passed, the undergrowth holding in the oppressive heat and humidity.

For the time, caution and care were lifted. Jennet pressed Bracken on, although in truth the sturdy little pony seemed possessed by the same glad calling that infected its mistress. That *he* would follow was not doubted. Stumbling and sick and frightened for her, he would come. A momentary wonder touched her that such as she could ever inspire such a response in any living being, then she pushed even that back, back behind her carefully constructed defenses. She would not yield. She would not.

Aedan saw the hood slip from her head, saw the stretch of the pony's neck as they splashed through a runlet washing across the trail. Trail... this was a well-worn path on the way to somewhere. He had, after all, wished to come down out of the mountains into the valleys, and so they had, but not to any valley he had ever known.

Dobbet's small hooves made no sound as they sank into lush green grass that edged the valley forests. Vivid blue trumpets of blossoms vined about the trunks of smooth-barked trees. Cascades of fluted yellow, lavender, and shell-pink flowers fell in garlands from the lower forest canopy. Aedan loosened his cloak and pushed back his sleeves. Jennet was lost to sight, but he felt her presence near at hand. The tie that bound them still held. Water ran at their feet, and bejeweled insects spluttered from grass and bush as they passed. Clouds of birds as bright as any blossom started at the shrill whicker of Dobbet, an unseen Bracken answering. Rounding a massive, solitary tree, heavy with mosses and fruit-bearing vines, Aedan found himself in a clearing. Jennet stood, listening, by the side of a pool, then sudden as a wink disappeared.

"Jennet!" The cry was torn from him as he swung free of the pony. "Jennet!"

Behind him, a low-throated laugh sounded. Aedan swung about. Jennet smiled at him, her eyes wide with pleasure and delight, and then she was gone again. Aedan stared, swinging about as he heard her laugh once more behind him. As he turned, he caught only the flicker of movement as she did her disappearing trick again.

"Play your game, then, Jennet," he called out at last, pulled his pack from Dobbet, and led the pony to the pool. Tired and distressed, he sank to his knees, dousing his face and then whole head with water. Whatever game she played, he was too tired to care.

A crisp cheerful blaze popped and crackled, shooting small sparks that arced and flared away to ash as Aedan watched. A twig snapped behind him, and Jennet stepped around the fire and sank onto her pack. Her face shone with a wild, spent happiness. She seemed sated, her gaze drawn inward, her lips stained from the juice of some fruit she'd eaten. Her hair tumbled and tangled about her shoulders. She gave a huge, sudden yawn, like a child.

Aedan tossed the dregs of his supper into the fire. Jennet was already dragging her cloak behind her. Snapping out the blanket before him, Aedan pulled another from his pack as Jennet dropped to her knees, bundled her cloak into a clumsy pillow, and curled herself into a ball, asleep before he drew the second blanket over her. How long he sat listening to the songs of frogs and night-singing insects, he did not know, but at last he turned his back to the smoldering coals and slept.

'Aedan.'

Her voice woke him from a heavy, troubled sleep.

'Aedan, come! See how the stars glitter, calling out to us! Lift your senses to the sweet perfumes that entice us from sleep. Come, Aedan, wake!'

Aedan struggled against the hold of sleep and rubbed his eyes. Jennet lay sprawled easily against him, lips parted, a faint sheen of warmth caressing her cheek. Aedan stared. She was sound asleep.

'Aedan! Aedan, please!'

He closed his eyes in confusion. Jennet's face rose before him—her eyes wide, hair tumbling anyhow about her shoulders. He opened his eyes quickly. Jennet lay as before. Tentatively, he reached out a finger to stroke the tresses from her cheek. She slept on, turning her face into his touch. Trembling, Aedan snatched his hand away.

"Oh, Jennet!" He barely breathed the words. "What tumult plays havoc with your defenses, leaving this inner Jennet to cajole me from my sleep? I could love you as you sleep unwary, and you would have me eagerly.

"And yet... and yet!"

He could not leave her, for they were bound together. How could he stay? He who was only human and wanted her with every fiber of his being, body and soul? Aedan turned from the sight of her and took a deep breath. Under his breath, he began to recite the beginning of the *Quoran Dru*, a highly intricate verse-poem by that last mythical prophet who had roamed the valleys and the mountains ages past. He'd found the translation among his father's papers, learning it by heart as if to assuage the grief of his father's death.

The high-born seeks a path to loneliness.
Loneliness, like a stone, is cold and heavy.
Yet, look closer. When warmed by sun
And worn by water, a stone may become
A thing of beauty. This is the first

Observation of the Quoran Dru.

Aedan closed his mind against her treacherous whisper. If she would not come to him awake with all her senses joined, he would not take advantage of a false illusion of love or desire.

Jennet woke with the dawn, rubbing eyes as heavy as though drugged. Dully, she looked about her. Aedan lay stretched on his back beside her—sleeping the sleep of exhaustion, even now lines of strain etching the planes of his face.

The dreams she'd had! Jennet blushed to think of them. What was this place? Like she'd come home, recognition had surged from some level of memory beyond conscious recall. All cares had seemed far away, scattered like lailiki blossoms in late summer. She gulped. She had dreamed of Aedan. She had touched him in her dream, cajoled him and yet now—with certainty she knew that it had not been a dream. As she stared at him, eyes narrowed, she saw that he had not the look of a sated lover. Anger shook her for a moment, before she checked herself at the irony of it all. How could she be angry that he'd resisted her charms? Or, angry that he'd been honorable? The last thing she wanted, she admitted to herself, was another facet of his character revealed, building a grudging admiration and respect that she did not want to feel?

"Come." She nudged Aedan with the tip of her boot and could not bring herself to say his name as he stirred, "come, we must be on our way."

Aedan rolled a wary, haunted look at her, and sudden shame filled her. Those lines of stress, put there by her own foolishness. What was this place?

"Come," a note of panic edged her voice. "Hurry, Aedan!" His head snapped up sharply as his name slipped out unawares.

Jennet once more led the way, Aedan following, alert and silent. Where they rode, following the stream, it was cool and shady. The stream flowed, steadily widening. A fever pitch of expectancy built in the very air around them. Great red and blue and emerald green parrots and white-crested cockatoos started up at their passage. Unseen animals hooted and called above them, the animals' cries resounding and echoing through the forest. Aedan pressed Dobbet closer to Jennet. The ponies were equally keyed up, their pace quickening until they were galloping along the path.

A dull roar penetrated the understory of the rainforest. A vine slashed and caught at them, slowing Dobbet as Aedan almost tumbled from his mount. Swearing breathlessly, he pushed Dobbet forward. In just that space of a second, Jennet was fast disappearing from sight. Faster and faster he urged his pony. The roar increased to a thunderous booming—the cacophony unendurable. The stream had long since been swollen by a complicated network of feeders into a rushing torrent. The trees thinned as Aedan came pounding down the trail after Jennet.

"Jennet!" His cry was useless. Had she heard, he doubted if she would slow. Bracken burst into the clearing at a full gallop, Aedan right behind on Dobbet. The river rushed headlong over a precipice before them, the force of its fall spraying foam high into the air.

Jennet abruptly reined in Bracken and threw herself free. Aedan catapulted from his own mount and raced after her. He never understood the impulse that caused him to reach for her hand, leaping with her well out into space above the falls, rocks splintered and glittering like frozen glass shards green and brilliant far below. It seemed to Aedan that they hung suspended forever, then light, sound, consciousness were swept away.

Chapter 3

Barak tapped the side of his nose with a finger. Obal stepped out of the shadow of a clump of elms, his cloaked shadow seeming to move without source past the wan light that flickered at the side of a rickety gate. Once Obal had fastened the gate behind him, Barak settled himself comfortably, keeping a clear view of the lane which ended at this gate and the path leading from it into the patches of mist which covered an overgrown, neglected garden within the walls.

Carrig's breath warmed the crystals held loosely in his hand, then he threw them like dice onto the cloth-covered table before him. When the echoes of their falling, like chimes, died away, he stared intently into the maze of crystalline planes that reflected back the flames from the fireplace which was the only source of light in the room. As Obal watched, the crystals began to clear. Within them, images appeared, flickered, and disappeared.

Other images came, some lingered and on another facet, another image formed. Obal saw snow falling in mountains—gray peaks slashed at a clouded, cheerless sky. A group of dark-robed figures formed a semi-circle. A leaf fell as if past an open window. A dying campfire lit a formless, blanket-covered shape. The images dissolved and reformed faster and faster. A pony stamped uneasily beside a stream bank. Bright birds started in flight. A young woman slept a troubled, uneasy sleep. One brown hand reached for and captured a small, pale hand.

Obal jerked at the image. Carrig raised a brow. Obal mopped his forehead and peered again into the crystals. Their facets dimmed, then cleared to reveal one scene fractured into a thousand glimmering fragments. Hooded, bowed figures stood, linked each to each, and each one holding a candle. Hood after hood fell back as the figures straightened, with each grim, set face staring at some focus beyond sight. What or who they watched remained unseen.

In the next instant, without a breath of air stirring in the room, the images were gone, the crystals reflecting back only the flames flickering on Carrig's hearth.

"Well?" Barak asked, keeping his voice low. He and Obal were seated in the far corner of an ill-lit eatery, one where the well-scrubbed sons of the lower class ate their evening meal in boisterous groups. A few wayfarers were scattered here and there across the room. The food was plain, but plentiful, and the local ale sufficient to wash it down. Barak nudged Obal out of a brown study. "You are sure?"

"I tell you, I saw it as plain as that beak of a nose upon your face." Obal grinned at Barak, "That squared garnet caught in wild gold—the ring as clear upon that hand as it was lying still on the coverlet when we left him asleep in Taavel. And he wasn't alone. He was clasping the hand of a woman, I'd swear to it!" The big man paused, pushed back his plate, and stared in perplexity at his companion before continuing.

"So we know he's not alone, wherever he may be. And what's more, I think someone else is interested in his whereabouts as well." At Barak's sharp glance, Obal lowered his voice and hastened to explain.

"No, no, my friend, not *them*." Obal threw a quick look about the room, as if the mere thought of the Sindren Corps could conjure up its presence. "Besides them," he corrected himself, then proceeded to tell Barak of the silent hooded figures seen in the crystals.

The little man sat without speaking for several moments, eyes narrowed.

"Tell me, O Shaggy One, have you ever been to the shores of the Altari Sea?"

Obal chewed on a hunk of bread as he thought, then his broad features split into a smile. He reached across the table to clap Barak heartily on the shoulder.

"Trust you! What a mind for persnickety details! It's been well-nigh thirty years. Long e'er we came to the holding, eh?"

"Yes, my friend. And your eyes so bloodshot, your head so thick with drink then, I'm amazed you're able to dredge up any recollection of that place." Barak lowered his voice once more. "Do you also recall the lights flickering along the shoreline, growing as we watched into a circle of light at the water's edge? And only when the moon rose, did we see those curiously still figures, hooded and quiet as death itself." He shivered with the memory and took a gulp of his ale.

"Toss a few coppers to the serving boy. We'll be on our way."

Obal stood even as Barak spoke. A good five hours of riding in the middle of the night would make a good start—then a few hours of sleep somewhere out the way. They spoke little during their travels, keeping off the main roads, following trails, country lanes, and forest rides, but always making roughly south and east. A few hours before dawn, they found a sheltered copse where they could tether the horses and rest. By dawn they had risen and mingled with other traffic on the roads as farmers and tradesmen headed about their morning business.

Neither spoke of the fact that they were riding into a rakar snake's nest of the Sindren Corps—much too close for comfort if one dwelled on the prospect. Yet now, if they lost Aedan, would it matter any longer?

Barak whistled an aimless little tune under his breath, sipping now and then at his drink. By attaching themselves to a small traveling amusement show, he and Obal had passed across the shadow of the Almeridian coastal plain without incident. They had come by easy stages to the port of Altari-Maro—the city that sang by the sea. Altari-Maro was a city of merchants, perched between the Empire and the vast eastern holdings that remained closed to the West and the Empire's rule.

The city consisted of two parts. The Lower City was carefully laid out in broad avenues and narrow alleys. Two- and three-story mudbrick dwellings turned high, windowless walls to the world and looked inward for the comfort and privacy of their residents. From the outside it was impossible to tell what the standard of living might be within. Drains caught rainwater and wastewater, keeping the city dry and clean, unlike many of its Western counterparts. An outsider could easily become lost in this part of the city, with no landmarks to distinguish one street from another.

Beyond the lower city rose the citadel or Upper City. In this smaller portion of the city, great public baths and halls stood, as well as the marketplace, the granary, the library, and the hall of commerce. Great pitch-lined docks thrust into the river and emptied landward onto busy wharves where finished wares like textiles and bronzeware were shipped out by night and day. Here too cargoes of raw materials arrived hourly—fragrant oils, gleaming dark woods, and smaller, more precious stones and metals that found their way into the workshops which lined the marketplace or were sent on from Altari-Maro to Western artisans.

The city thronged with seamen and merchants, bankers, and drifters from all parts of the Empire. Here and there the throng would part to allow the passage of black-robed Corpsmen, whose shaven heads all perspired alike beneath the merciless sun. And interspersed among the masses of sailors and foreign traders, unobtrusively but with a subtle sense of vitality and strength, were the people of Altari-Maro.

Legend had it that they were called after the city in which they lived because, when questioned, it seemed they had no name for themselves. Even today, the strange, emblematic writing which they employed to account for their trade ventures and revenues remained indecipherable to outsiders. That they were allowed to operate on the fringes of the Empire without being wholly swallowed up by the Sindren Corps was due to this lack of a strong national pride and to another curious lack in their culture.

For neither in the Upper City nor the Lower City were there erected any public structures which could be construed as religious houses of worship. Within their dwellings were constructed no altars, no niches for statues of deities or other objects of worship, no cupboards to hold holy relics. No shrines adorned the countryside about the city. And in this lack, the Sindren Corps judged that no threat existed to their doctrines. The people of Altari-Maro were merchants and artisans through and through, untroubled by idolatrous or blasphemous thoughts.

So were the thoughts that passed through Barak's mind as he sat within the cool recesses of the courtyard. He stopped whistling and sipped his drink, meditatively watching the abstract patterns of shadow and light form, break, then reform as a light breeze and the barest trickle of water in a fountain disturbed the shimmering blue pool at the heart of Isman-Bati's garden. Isman-Bati, the cloth merchant who had welcomed the two of them. He bought from and sometimes sailed with some of the Eastern ships, selecting wondrous fine silks and cottons to be dyed and woven in his workshops. These were staffed from weaver guilds, positions in the workshops zealously guarded and passed from generation to generation. Isman-Bati's father had been a cloth merchant, and his father before him. For as long as anyone could remember, the family had prospered as cloth merchants.

Turning back to the scene behind him, Barak caught sight of Assir, the eldest Bati son, and Obal, both relaxed on bright cushions, laughing at some jest from Assir. A dark, thin girl, sinuous as the gold bracelet curled about her forearm, danced before them. The patterns of the music to which she moved with grace subtly changed and in that change, the girl's pace altered so that it seemed as if her feet answered to the music's direction and its call, without conscious thought on the dancer's part.

Barak shifted in his seat. *Pattern....* He started as Isman-Bati laid a hand on his shoulder.

"Come, my friend." The merchant's dark eyes gleamed with amusement and mock concern. "What troublous thoughts burden you that you should scowl so black in my garden of delights?"

"I was thinking, Isman-friend, that if I were to close my eyes, some pattern of life that lies beneath the surface of Altari-Maro would be revealed to me."

Barak kept his voice light, but glanced sharply at his friend as he spoke. He could swear the dark eyes widened in surprise. A laugh—a shade too loud? Too long?—gave his host a moment's hesitation before he replied.

"Barak, you have been too long in the sun! But, of course there is a pattern here. There are many patterns here! Have you forgotten that this is a house filled with weavers?" The man laughed, inviting Barak to share the joke. "Come, let us have more of this excellent young wine and some fruit before the night grows long."

Isman-Bati took Barak's arm. As they moved towards the light and reached the curtained canopy of the inner courtyard, he spoke in a casual tone.

"Perhaps sometime, Barak-friend, when it is clear which pattern you seek, Isman-Bati may be able to help."

Bathing in the Great Bath, Obal shook himself like a large, wet bear and grumbled contentedly deep in his throat as he toweled himself dry. In the next cubicle, Assir was singing in his own language. Simple and repetitive, the tune might have been a child's song. As Obal dressed, he found himself humming the little tune. Pulling his tunic over his head, he turned about to find Barak lounging against the doorframe. The big man gave a sheepish grin at the smirk on his comrade's face.

"Catchy little tune, eh my friend? I wonder what the words mean?"

"Catchy, indeed," Barak agreed with a nod. "Why don't you ask Assir what it means?"

They walked with Assir to the wharves, where a worker held a cart before a ship. Isman-Bati had purchased some quantities of fine cotton from the ship's captain. Once the cart was loaded, they would accompany the driver to the artisans' quarter. To account for their presence in the city, Barak and Obal had concocted a cover that they were exploring a possible partnership with the cloth merchant. To that end, it was needful to make a show of looking at the merchandise from start to finish—a show which also allowed them to move about the city as they searched for some sign of the dark-robed group seen in Carrig's crystals.

"And learning more," Obal remarked in an aside to Barak, "than ever I wished to know about where my clothes began!"

Barak found the final step—the actual weaving—fascinating. The weavers—both male and female, old and young—worked from an image in their head or else made up the pattern as it pleased them, for nowhere were designs drawn out. And no two patterns were ever exactly the same. Highly abstracted designs were built by skillful hands and eyes hour after hour, day after day. Other weavers produced life-like scenes of river flowers, mountain grasses, and detailed reproductions of birds, small creatures, and indigenous insects—like the great iridescent moths that appeared only before moonrise. Oxen in profile peered from long rough goods—even these lovely enough to grace some Western noble's wall.

"But, see," Obal observed to Barak as they left the weaver's workshops, "no human figures anywhere in all that work." Nor, in the days which followed, were any to be seen in any of the other shops they visited within Al-tari-Maro.

Barak walked beside Assir or Isman-Bati on their journeys about the city, asking no questions, but engrossed in everything he saw, committing all to his prodigious memory. The little man was often silent now, as if all his energy were directed at some interior train of thought. He had the feeling—one he couldn't quite put into words yet—that all these details of life in the city would provide him with an answer, or answers, or perhaps the knowledge to frame the proper questions he needed to put to Isman-Bati. They had been in the city a month now—he could almost feel some awareness growing within himself.

One evening they sat at table with Isman-Bati and his family. Besides the eldest, Assir, Isman had four younger sons—Taki, Samna, Sherat, and Joghar, and two daughters—Bahri and Kapura—all dark-eyed and merry like their mother. Mari-Isman's perpetual look of harried amusement deepened into affection whenever her gaze lingered on any of her children or her husband. Obal sat as relaxed as sap running in the first spring sun. Mari, her daughters, and the younger two sons prepared and served the meal.

Like all other evening meals he and Barak had shared in Isman's home, this one began with a thimbleful of clear, subtle tea which was followed by baskets of crisp lentil flatbreads served with aromatic dips with pungent, spicy sauces. Talk ebbed and flowed as the assembled family members and guests helped themselves.

As the last crumbs were being wiped from the corners of mouths, Bahri and Kapura carried a steaming samovar of rice to table and served each person on a warmed, finely-glazed plate. Sherat and Joghar followed their mother in, she laden with a huge platter—sometimes of fish or other fruits of the sea's harvest; other nights fowl or pork might be prepared. This night, some of each was presented as small cubes cooked quickly. The platter sat in the middle of the table over warming bricks. The sons placed bowls of crisp green shoots, red peppers, yellow squashes, and other vegetables around the platter of meats. Isman poured out the wine as each person served themselves.

As the days passed, Obal found himself looking forward to this shared meal more and more. With the wine and full plates, and each person urging others to taste this or that morsel, conversation generally lagged until the end of the meal. At last fresh fruits and small, rich sweets were offered along with elaborate cups of a strong, dark drink produced in the southern hills. Obal sighed with contentment. He took a sip of his brew, accepted a honey-drenched square of pastry from Kapura, and surveyed his table companions. What a soothing, comforting rhythm ran through this company!

Obal bit harder than he intended into his pastry, spraying crumbs onto his beard. Yes! Sherat and Kapura were humming that pretty little tune under their breaths—the one he'd overheard Assir singing that day in the baths. It occurred to him that he'd approached this meal as a man to his devotions—that the elaborate meal-time was as carefully planned and orchestrated as any religious service he'd ever attended.

His glance took in Isman, Mari-Isman, and their children. All were smiling gently, Isman and Mari with hands clasped, both parents and their children picking up the tune and singing softly. Even Barak, he noted, hummed with the rest. For himself, he sat back in his chair, a huge, satisfied grin spreading across his features.

Early the following morning, as Barak sat alone, breaking his fast by the edge of the courtyard fountain, Obal reached over his shoulder to take a warm chunk of bread from Barak's plate, smearing it liberally with honey. Chewing thoughtfully, he savored the warm sweetness of his morning meal.

"Tell me, Barak," he began at length, "is this not a breakfast fit for the gods?"

"Yes, you happy convert, it is indeed a heavenly repast." Barak moved the plate of bread closer to his friend.

"No! No—you mistake my meaning," Obal spoke with mock reproach, then tapped the bread before him, his features earnest. "It struck me, this evening past, that our dinner was in itself like an act of worship." He stumbled to a halt, groping for words. "Do you not feel it, Barak? That we partake of something larger than its parts—the food, the hungry children—serving and sharing?" As Barak raised a brow at him, but did not speak, Obal shrugged.

"Perhaps it's just my stomach, feeding my imagination, no?"

"Oh no! Obal, you may be a great hungry bear of a man, but I think you've found but part of a pattern.

"Think you of the weavers and the potters and the jewelers and the smiths. Think of the tidy careful fields stretching beyond the city. Think of the day and the orchestrated cadences of everyday life—how the inhabitants of Altari-Maro go each morning to the baths, each evening to home and hearth and family."

"Of the Lower and the Upper City," Obal added, his eyes gleaming.

"Faith and devotion color the very air here, Obal. It's all around us, not fragmented into separate rigid compartments, or people, or buildings. No wonder the Corps," he spat, "has always been surrounded by it and did not notice! I think, Obal, that it's time to speak with Isman-Bati. Those hooded figures in the night—he may know what we seek to find."

"If," Obal cautioned his friend, "he's willing to speak."

Isman sat behind his wife as her deft fingers wove a single strand the color of sunlight on a new leaf into the tapestry taking shape on her loom. Obal and Barak waited patiently until Isman saw them and rose to join them.

"Ho, my friends, is Mari-Isman's work not lovely?" He gestured proudly at his wife. Simultaneous nods of assent answered him. "Shall we walk?" Their host indicated the dim recesses of the courtyard.

"What was it that you saw, friends, which brought you to Altari-Maro after so long a time? What need drove you to return to our fair city?"

The calm directness of his queries caught them by surprise, then Barak clapped his friend on the shoulder and laughed at himself.

"Well, go on, Obal! Tell Isman of our youthful drunken revels on that last long-ago trip to Altari-Maro—after we left his household and were on our wandering way again."

"And so," Isman remarked as Obal finished his tale, "you felt the need of spiritual enlightenment and returned to our city to seek it?" He continued with the hint of a smile at the look which passed between his companions, "No? There is yet more to be told?"

"Let us be seated, Isman-Bati, friend," Barak took a deep breath. "We will tell you of a child now lost—or perhaps not lost at all."

They seated themselves under a shaded bower in the depths of the courtyard. As at some unseen signal from his father, Joghar brought them tea and plates of thin wafers and withdrew. Barak turned his cup about in his hands. Obal stared into his tea, not seeing it, lost in thought. Barak met the mild, curious gaze of Isman.

"Obal and I, Isman-Bati, as you well know, were wild young rovers in our youth, serving no lord or master save the whims of the moment. One journey brought us tired and depleted of funds to the holding of Mikal the Scholar on the River Severn in the province of Halfern.

"Obal being stalwart and cunning with sword and knife and myself," he added with feigned modesty, "being a good hand with the mounts, we thought to work for some time and accrue enough in payment to send us on our way again."

"Aye," Obal glanced up from his cup. "Mikal was a decent, honest man, giving fair wages and a generous founding of room and board."

"He was a man of his books, true to his name," Barak continued, "but not removed from this world, you see, Isman. Rather, he was well-content to pursue his life's work and rest the running of the holding in the hands of his steward, Zaavan."

At the man's name, Obal's eyes narrowed and his face flushed darkly. His large hands squeezed his cup. He seemed unmindful of the pottery shards and dripping tea until Bahti, appearing with a towel, loosed his fingers, and took away the ruined cup.

Barak, his thin lips tightening, went on.

"Mikal was preoccupied when we came to the holding. His wife Anja was great with their first child. Not long after our arrival, she gave birth to a son—Aedan."

"A fairer child you never saw," Obal spoke with pride.

Barak and Isman exchanged a glance.

"But, 'twas true, Isman. Aedan grew into a curious, radiant child with laughter to make a man's heart sing. We grew to love him and because he seemed taken with us,

Anja urged Mikal to set us as his tutors for such skills and arts he could not get from his father's books."

"So you remained at the holding," Isman interjected when Barak paused.

"Aye, so it came to pass, Isman. One year followed after another—" he broke off as Obal jumped up and blundered away, pacing like a caged bear. Isman lifted his eyes to the balcony above the courtyard. The quick, light patter of feet sounded on the stairs into the courtyard. Isman and Mari's brood swarmed about Obal, cajoling him to join them. Bahri produced a board and Sherat the playing pieces. Kapura and Samna each took one of Obal's great hands and between them all, drew him off to a sun-splashed corner of the courtyard where they settled themselves on cushions.

Barak sighed and turned to Isman-Bati, keeping his voice low.

"We loved the boy, and Mikal and Anja treated us well. Obal took a fancy to a local woman—the lorewoman's daughter Ilissa—and married. The boy was a joy to teach, Isman. He was disciplined and careful in his dealings with the horses, and yes," Barak conceded with the ghost of a grin, "even with the people who surrounded him—adults, playmates, all. Only with Zaavan did he keep his distance.

"When he was nine years' old, winter came early and hard to the holding. Anja caught a chill that would not heal. She grew worse as winter lingered. Mikal was beside himself. At length, he sent for us one night.

"Anja was wrapped in blankets, and Mikal himself dressed for travel. He charged us with the care of Aedan, saying he intended to seek help for his wife. Anja stirred and woke at her name, and seeing her husband dressed thusly, pleaded with us to stop him.

"Mikal was frantic. There was, he told us, one chance to heal her—to find a 'City of Light,' where her people lived. They would be able to save her. He saw our glances and knew we thought him mad with worry. He seemed to take hold of himself and calmed his wife.

"It was then he confided in us that Anja was not as the ordinary folk of the holding. She was come from the mountains in some resettlement forced by the Empire, a woman with a spirit free as a bird, light as a moth on the wind.

"Some among her people had eluded the Empire's forces and settled somewhere in the mountains. Word had come, somehow, that such a refuge existed. People seeking a way to this place would travel into the mountains and might wake to find that a companion had vanished. Slowly, carefully, this point of no return had been tracked.

"Mikal meant to try—in the dead of winter—to reach this pass in the Naransai Mountains. But at this, Anja spoke clearly, beseeching her husband to send her off with only one man to guide her. For the sake of their son, she begged him to stay for Aedan's sake.

"Almost as if, Isman, she foresaw her future. For at length, much against his will, Mikal was persuaded. Obal offered to guide her, and I, to keep close watch on Aedan, and truth to tell, though I did not say it, on Mikal as well."

Barak turned his cup about in his hands, then sighed.

"It came to pass, nearly a month was gone when Obal returned alone. Mikal emerged from his rooms where he had been shut up for days—mourning. Obal could say only that a woman met them one night on the trail. This woman helped him nurse Anja, whose cough had worsened. Obal, in spite of himself, fell asleep sometime in the night. Morning came and Anja and the woman were gone. Obal could find no sign of them, and after several forlorn days of futile casting about, set out in despair for the holding.

"After that, Mikal withdrew ever more deeply into his books. He kept a watchful eye upon his son, but all else escaped him. This lack of oversight pleased Zaavan. He took more and more control, taking it upon himself to make decisions that once only Mikal could have ordered and others his master would never have sanctioned. And, in time, was challenged by Aedan, who made his father see what had come to pass.

"I see," Isman murmured, taking Barak's cup and refilling it. "And this tale leads here, to Altari-Maro?"

Barak shook his head.

"Yes, for us, Isman. Mikal was aghast at what Zaavan had done. He ordered him from the holding. The look that man sent at Aedan—a lad of only twelve then, who'd had the courage to stand up to him!

"Life was more normal after that. By the time he was sixteen, Aedan ran the holding on his father's word. Understand me, Isman—grown men cheerfully took his direction and followed his orders. He was old for his years, I think, when he was born.

"Bear with me, friend, for this tale draws to an end. Mikal, out riding alone, was stricken in a fall when Aedan had become a young man. Mikal never regained consciousness and died upon the morn. Two days later Zaavan came riding into the holding, a troop of black-robed, sour-faced monks on all sides.

"He claimed the holding in the name of the Sindren Corps. Aedan—full of fury for once—full of grief for his father newly buried—demanded to know under what authority Zaavan did so. Zaavan held a proclamation before him and read how he had been appointed guardian for Aedan, who had neither father nor mother nor any other relative to speak for him. Furthermore, he read on, said mother—assumed deceased—had been proven blasphemous and an evil in the eyes of the Empire. Her only offspring would be placed under the care of a friend of the court until it could be shown that he was not tainted by the same wickedness.

"Aedan sprang at the man. Zaavan lashed out at him with his crop. Obal, roaring like a derval bull in a monsoonal frenzy, charged to the rescue, many of the holding's men following. The Corps flanked their leader and drew lieber-sabers. The men checked, all save Obal, who placed himself between Aedan and Zaavan. Myself, I reached Aedan's side and restrained him.

"Zaavan barked a series of orders. The monks rounded up the holding's women and children. Zaavan gestured. Ilissa—Obal's wife—just swelling with their first child—was dragged forth. Obal threw himself at her, but the lieber-saber struck her before ever he reached her. She died in his arms."

Isman-Bati bowed his head, weary and saddened. A moment of silence passed between the two friends.

"Aedan and I took Obal to a small valley in the north of the holding. There we shepherded the winter flocks, and Obal slowly rallied as we strove to keep Aedan from Zaavan's sight. It seemed, almost, that the man had forgotten our very existence in the next year until a few months before Aedan would have stood to title as the owner of the holding. Then word came to bring him to Zaavan or else.

"We brought him and were dismissed from the holding. Obal and I went quickly, but not far. The Corps and Zaavan were not much loved, and word was got to us that Aedan had taken ill. A strange sickness that made him speak of visions seemingly conjured by his fever. But Zaavan had the Sindren priests poke and prod him until they pronounced him the offspring of his mother and not fit to serve either temple or holding."

The cloth merchant's lips curled in understanding. Such a proclamation meant death.

"Babil, Aedan's old nurse, blind in the laundry, contrived to send word to us. Loyal women and men of the holding smuggled him from the holding's manor house to an outlying farm. Obal and I took him from there. Remembering Mikal's words from long ago, we tried to retrace Obal's journey with Anja into the Naransai, avoiding the wrath of Zaavan and the Corps as we went. By cautious stages, we came at last to Taavel. Aedan's illness grew worse as we journeyed, and we left him, securely we thought, while we sought to make sure we'd covered our trail. Aedan disappeared without a trace from the city."

Barak picked up his cup, put it down again, and looked up at his friend.

"At wits' end, we sought the services of Carrig, the crystal-reader. And what was seen in his crystals, Isman, brought us to you. Is it possible, friend-Bati, that the City of Light found Aedan?"

Chapter 4

A concentrated, fierce heat woke him. Aedan blinked. A shutter, loosely fastened, had come open in a passing spasm of the intermittent breeze, allowing the strong morning rays of the sun to cross his face as he lay abed. Aedan sat up abruptly, memory flooding his mind. Jennet?! Wildly, he looked about, taking in the spare frame bed canopied with translucent, fine nettings in which he lay. Beside him, the bed was empty. His eyes narrowed and he fumbled with the netting, pushing it aside. The pillow beside his own was untouched, nor had the bed the look of a second occupant. Where was Jennet? The tie between them, to her continued and silent outrage, could not be broken. Unless? Aedan halted, his hand gripping the doorknob—if not in life, then in death?

He jerked the door open with a sudden, searing desperation, finding before him a timbered verandah running around a courtyard below. No sign of life was evident, save for the casual twitch of the tail by a ginger-colored cat—its queer triangular face nuzzled between its forepaws, eyes closing in a lazy dismissal of this insignificant intrusion. It lay in a huge pot of flowers at the top of a flight of steps that led down into the interior of the courtyard. Without hesitating, Aedan headed down to the courtyard level. About the upper verandah were set a dozen or more doors identical to his own. He knew without wasting precious moments exploring that Jennet was not to be found behind any of them.

The stone-tiled courtyard felt cool beneath his bare feet. He caught a glimpse of himself in a sculpted jewel of a pool that lay at the center of the space. His upper body was brown and bare and muscled, not large-boned but sinewy, the garnet on his left hand gleaming as it caught a stray ray of sunlight, his lower body encased in some gauzy white trousers caught below the waist and above the ankles with supple leather thongs.

Aedan struck out across the courtyard towards an ornate arched opening in the north wall, seeing no one, hearing nothing that indicated the presence of any other living being.

Stopping short within the archway, he saw that it gave upon a vast colonnaded chamber. Soft light fell in pools upon the floor, diffusing from clerestory openings set high above the columns. Nothing graced this space except for a dais set three steps above the floor at the far end of the room. No furnishings broke it up, no tapestries enlivened the bare stone and timber construction of the walls, no rugs either covered the floor or directed the feet or eyes to any particular portion of the space.

And yet, in the play of light and shadow, in the rhythms of the breezes which moved between the columns, a harmony tugged at Aedan—a ceaseless weav-

ing of something as hypnotic as Sindren chanting, something palpable.

In the heart of silence, music lives.
To hear, the high-born must seek the path
Along which the taut string quivers,
Plucking music from the air, from water,
From the wind. This is the second
Observation of the Quoran Dru.

The verse came unbidden to his lips. Aedan found
himself repeating it aloud, over and over, as he took one
step, and then another toward the dais. As he stared into
the dim recesses of the chamber, the play of light and
shadow seemed to take substance. Row upon row of dark-
clad figures swayed among the columns, linked hand to
hand, the link broken only along the aisle before him, the
lines closing rank behind him as he approached the dais.

This time, unlike in his fevered dreams, the figures before him held, were solid and real. Aedan halted. Before
him, one figure stood isolated upon the dais, hood pushed
back to reveal an ancient woman, ageless in the clear-eyed
gaze with which she observed him. Four figures stepped
forward to flank him, two to the right and two to the left.

"Aedan Q'tar," the woman's voice rang out strong and
precise, "we bid thee welcome to Abri-Hataro—the City of
Light!"

Five heads bowed in unison before her and a breeze
seemed to sweep through the rows behind him.

"Like thy mother before thee, may thou rejoice in the
Light!" She stretched forth her hands to Aedan. As he

grasped for her outstretched hands, he felt himself to be the focus of an intense, concentrated surge of emotion and power—power of a kind he had never encountered before. The soles of his feet vibrated against the floor. Hair stood up along his neck. As if struggling against a great inertia, Aedan lifted his hands in response to that greeting. Slowly, slowly, with all his will and might he strove to reach those outstretched hands. Their fingertips touched. For an instant, a tremendous sense of comfort enveloped him, followed by a shock which ran through him. As he closed his eyes against the shock, he was aware of sinking to his knees, the ancient gray eyes above him wide with surprise and a shock of their own. Then, an arm came about his shoulders from his left—Jennet! On unsteady legs, he opened his eyes and stood. Hand in hand he faced the old woman with Jennet at his side. She waved her arm before her.

"Leave us."

Once more, like the winking out of a candle's flame, the throng which filled the hall was gone. Jennet remained, as did the three other figures with whom Jennet had stood.

"Miak, Dilys." The two so named—a fair-haired young man no older than Aedan and a fiery-haired, lithe young woman—stepped forward from Aedan's right to each side of the woman who commanded them. The third figure, a man of middle years, moved to stand behind Aedan and Jennet.

"Come, I wish to retire to my quarters. Patar Q'an, thou shall accompany the Q'tar and await my command." She moved with evident difficulty to the far edge of the dais. A doorway appeared there in response to a negligent flip of her wrist. When they were gone—the door with them, Patar Q'an smiled gently at Aedan and Jennet.

"You, Aedan Q'tar, must be hungry. Let us find sustenance and a quiet corner of the city in which to walk and talk, yes?"

Dark hair cropped close to the sides revealed a scattering of gray about the temples and over the ears in the man's hair. Above, the hair lay in vigorous curls, spilling over a broad, furrowed forehead. He was taller than Aedan by a head, broad-shouldered with a deep tan. A second smile came and went, revealing white and gleaming teeth, as he turned without waiting for a reply. Patar Q'an wore trousers much like those in which Aedan found himself dressed, and over them a loosely woven robe of sea blue stripes. He shed his darker over-robe as they moved toward the courtyard, Jennet following suit. A slight youth materialized out of nowhere, collected the robes with a brilliant, insouciant grin, handed a loosely woven robe like Patar's to Aedan, and was gone in the same instant.

Shrugging into the robe, Aedan stared in bewilderment at Jennet. She had, he noticed in confusion, taken his hand again and now gave it a comforting squeeze. He felt all of six years' old and grinned at himself. What might have been an answering amusement twinkled momentarily in Jennet's eyes, before she pulled him along to catch up with Patar Q'an. They strode along a path set at an angle to the entrance to the colonnaded hall. A gate loomed before them and beyond, Aedan drank in the scene with fascination. An entire city, built of some gleaming, porous white stone, spread before them.

Women, dressed like Jennet with robes kilted onto overskirts or trousers like his own, and men—of all ages and sizes—rescued toddlers as they made precarious, jolting runs for freedom, carried bundles, formed loose-knit knots of laughter and gay conversation, or bickered amiably at open-air stalls. The stalls contained fresh arrays of produce, flowers, pottery, and a multitude of other goods and products that overflowed the stalls to spill upon the clean, tiled walks that surrounded the street on which Aedan stood gaping.

A half-dozen voices rang out as they passed. "Patar-friend, good-day to you!" "Jennet-beauty, come sing with us!" Open, inviting glances included Aedan in these comments.

At length Patar halted at a succession of stalls where he purchased small, round loaves of hard, black bread, soft white cheeses, and fresh slices of a deep red fruit. In a side street off the main market avenue, they found a tiny, shaded park consisting of a fountain with a statue of a lady, a patch of tiled courtyard, and four wooden benches. One was occupied by a dozing, elderly man, the second by a young man reading a dog-eared volume, and the third by two women sharing a meal similar to their own. Patar led the way to the fourth, unoccupied bench.

Aedan discovered that he was, indeed, famished. But even as he ate, he watched his two companions with care. Jennet and Patar ate in a companionable silence that spoke of the ease of long friendship between them. Yet Jennet, he was certain, had been as ignorant as he of the existence of this city. The City of Light, the old woman had named it. He could contain himself no longer, but addressed the lazy blue eyes of Patar Q'an.

"Where are we? Why were we brought here?"

Patar's blue eyes sharpened with amusement.

"You are in Abri-Hataro, Aedan Q'tar, the City of Light. You are here because you are the Q'tar."

Aedan flushed, looked at Jennet with an unspoken appeal. The amusement ill-hidden in Patar's eyes was not reflected in her gaze.

"Please," she turned to their companion, putting a hand on his arm, "he has a right to know, does he not?"

Patar Q'an sighed.

"Ah, the impetuousness of youth! Do not glare at me so, young Q'tar! I will tell you what I may.

"Abri-Hataro lies on the eastern slopes of the Singha Mountains. To the north, of course, lies the Empire. Around us a vast rainforest stretches to a great river—one you may have heard spoken of in legend perhaps—the Dura?"

As Aedan's eyes widened in involuntary disbelief, Patar continued.

"That explains where we are. As to why, why, because you are the Q'tar." He shrugged, palms up, as if the explanation should be self-evident.

"But!" At a quick, sideways shake of the head by Jennet, Aedan desisted. Despite Aedan's frustration, the man had told all he could or would tell for now. Patar stood and tossed the last crust of his bread to the birds twittering on the ground nearby.

"Come," he gestured Aedan and Jennet before him, "the heat grows. Let us return to the Abri-Corazon and rest."

Jennet covertly watched Aedan as Patar Q'an set a course back to the central hall, the open heart of the city. His eyes darted here and there, taking in the market street and its inhabitants, the finely wrought buildings that gleamed in the noonday sun, and the riotous growth that refused to be contained in tidy garden beds. Wide-eyed and lost in his thoughts, he stumbled over a curb. Without thinking, Jennet reached out a hand to steady him and felt the tremor that went through him at her touch. He did not turn to look at her, however, and for that she was grateful.

Once inside the Abri-Corazon courtyard again, Patar Q'an gestured to a dim interior hallway beneath the staircase down which Aedan had descended earlier. The passageway opened into a series of salons arranged about and screened from a smaller, quieter courtyard. From somewhere unseen, the plaintive notes of a strange bird's song fluted across the muted voices and occasional laughter that came from salons they passed. At length Patar Q'an stopped before a doorway.

"You may rest here, if you will. I will come when our lady wishes your presence." With a nod and a quick smile, he was gone.

The salon to which Patar had brought them was not, after all, empty. Cushioned divans and high-backed woven chairs were clustered about the room. Woven screens separated the seating areas. In one grouping, a small dark-haired woman strummed a gittern while a circle of bright-eyed children listed with rapt faces to the music.

Jennet drew Aedan to a solitary divan drawn close to a screen. She curled up on a corner cushion, Aedan settling across from her. How tired he looked! Jennet caught her breath as the thought struck her—by rights he should be dead!

"What?"

Jennet realized she must have spoken her thought aloud and a slow flush warmed her cheeks. She hastened to explain.

"No one comes here, Aedan, without seeking the way. No one can come into the City of Light without belonging." She held up a hand as he started to speak.

"No, listen to me, Aedan. I will not lead you about with double-talk.

"I am a child of the light—wish-born! My mother and my father also—born in a tiny mountain village where all were of the same people. Patar," she stumbled over the words in her haste, "Patar came from a neighboring village in the next high sliver of a valley. He knew my family. He says that it was much as it is here, in the City of Light, much poorer perhaps in material trappings, but equally joyous and light-hearted in our lives.

"But one day strangers came into the lower valleys—strangers who were of a solid, unimaginative nature. They did not dream or let their spirits rise gladly to meet us. Instead, they claimed our valleys for this thing called 'Empire.'

"They rounded up the people, those who demanded to know why we must suddenly tithe the greater part of the fruits of our efforts to this Empire. They came, led by glabrous, black-robed priests, and forced the villagers to take up what belongings they could grab before they were marched away.

"Two, three...fifty or more villages came together in this way and then these men, with their hard eyes and their papers and maps, pointed—'You and you and you.' Thus, they separated the people of each village into different groups and then marched each group off in separate directions." Her voice low and fierce, Jennet continued her tale.

"Whole villages were dispersed in this way. Entire families were often separated." She stopped, looking inward at the past as all the pain and despair of that time spilled into her present. Beside her, she felt Aedan stir. Looking up, she encountered his grave, steady gaze. He was not, she noticed, surprised by her story, but nodded as if it confirmed something already learned long ago.

"But, Jennet," his words came haltingly, as if he chose them with care, "here in Abri-Hataro, I have seen a hall filled with people disappear in the passing of a few seconds. How was it they could not escape the Empire?"

Pulling her robe about her as though suddenly chilled, Jennet could not keep the bitterness from her voice as she answered.

"They took the children, you see, from each family. In one of the first villages, a man... a man who had that much light within him, he thought, too, that he should simply go, his wife to follow and between the two of them, they could guide their child along the path of light.

"But the dark-robed men had taken hold of the child. When the parents disappeared before their eyes, they struck the child through with a dagger and left him in the village center to show how they dealt with demons and their offspring, for so they called these people." She stopped, choked, her voice coming as a whisper.

"That man was Patar Q'an, Aedan. His wife..." she gulped, her voice uneven and thread-bare as she forced out the rest of her tale, "she lost the path. It is worse than death. Her spirit wandering in the darkness and her body here, Aedan, dying without her so that Aisha is still lost—not alive on this earth, not wholly of the Light as spirit! Forever caught between!"

Aedan's hands closed about her own, chafing warmth back into them. She fought the impulse to bury herself in his arms, to hold him close and feel his heartbeat strong and steady beneath her ear, to feel safe and secure. She pulled her hands away, but with an unaccustomed gentleness, and tucked them under her crossed arms.

Aedan sat back, staring beyond the screen into the quiet courtyard for long moments. The strings of the gittern sounded a lilting melody, the children humming along. At length Aedan sighed and turned his gaze to Jennet once more.

"What of you, Jennet? Your family?"

"I never knew my parents. That is, I grew up on the higher slopes of the Naransai in a village of hardworking, sensible Burlen peasants. From the time I was old enough to notice, I marveled at how different I looked from my parents and my brothers, Yostl and Carli. All dark, heavy. Good, honest people, Aedan.

"Yostl was always solemn and grave, but he kept a special smile all for me and a polished red apple. Carli was a great jokester, always teasing me.

"But, I was not a very good daughter. I could not be trusted to watch the supper, for my mind would wander and the stew might burn. I could not weave, for I always wanted to weave bright, intricate patterns that took too much time. I could not work the fields because I was constantly distracted by the song of the light and the wind, the passage of a bird, the progress of a bug.

"I learned early on, Aedan, that I had this ability to be and not to be. As a child, I once tried to play hide and seek with my mother. She did not go out to seek me, but waited instead so patiently that I showed myself to her.

"She took me to the Elders then. And old Samma, the Eldest, told me to show her this trick. When I did and was back again, old Samma told me that I should never, ever do it again, for if word of it spread, I would be taken from my home by the dark-robed men who collected the tithes and that my mother and father and Yostl and Carli would suffer because of me.

"I could not understand why it was that I should be so different, you see. The Elders did not seek to explain, and I was much too frightened to ask."

"Yet, you risked everything to save my life, Jennet!" Aedan knew he'd made a mistake as soon as he spoke, but too late to take back his words. Jennet's eyes widened.

"No!" Jennet shook her head in immediate denial. She took a deep breath and exhaled slowly before speaking again. "You do not understand, Aedan. I did not choose to save you."

Frustration glittered in his eyes, but he forced himself to assume an even tone.

"I did not force you."

"I could not help myself," she cried, "because of what I am, because of who you are! Don't you realize, Aedan, that Mother, Father, Yostl, and Carli—they could have died if the Sindren had known what I did—and I did it without thought, without effort! It is only because the villagers loved me—different though I am—and closed ranks behind the Elders that I was allowed to live. As it is, I can never go back." She closed her eyes to squelch back the tears.

"Jennet, Jennet! Please, look at me!" Aedan implored, stretching a beseeching hand toward her. "Why or how it was that you saved me, I don't know. I knew you only in my dreams. I saw you running in a meadow, glowing to rival the sun! No wonder that the villagers loved you! But, I swear that I did not know that you were real or do anything knowingly to bind you to me."

Jennet recoiled, striking his hand away from her.

"Don't you think I live with that knowledge every blessed moment of my days?" she hissed, tears spilling from eyes huge with anger and a desperate sadness he could not fathom. She hugged her knees close to her body.

"Wait!" Aedan grasped her shoulder, "please, Jennet, don't go!"

She opened her eyes.

"Please," he removed his hand and sat back. "I can only say I'm sorry so many times. Help me to understand, Jennet, so that this tie between us may be ended and you can be free."

His words were soft, pleading. Jennet felt tears start to her eyes anew. She turned her head away so that Aedan would not see, sniffed once, but did not leave. How could she tell him what he had meant to her without hurting him further by showing him plainly how he had killed any chance of a future for them by his own confession? That she had given freely of that special part of herself, whom no one in her life had ever been able to share, only to know that *he* had not shared it purposefully, had not even known that she was real. She grasped her head in her hands.

Then she felt them, about the edges of her anguish—light soft touches like kisses or hugs. She opened her eyes in astonishment and turned to the children. The dark-haired woman with the gittern smiled at Jennet and Aedan.

"Come, Jennet," the children chorused, "sing with us! Come, Aedan, join our circle."

At once, Jennet slipped from her cushion and moved to sit among them. Two of the smaller ones grinned at her in welcome, one hugging her as the other child crawled into her lap and snuggled against her.

Behind her, Aedan hesitated. Concentrating upon the moth-like touches of warmth and concern that fluttered about the edges of recognition, he too sat down in the circle and found himself accepted as readily as Jennet. Two blond-haired charmers fell about his neck; he scooped them both up—both erupting into giggles—into his arms and sat them one on each knee. In that moment of laughter, it was as if a window opened in his mind. Light and laughter and love flooded in. Not thinking about it, but simply accepting it, Aedan felt a small dark core of pain that eased within him even as the song began. Now, larger, a taut-strung quiver of pain and anger began to relax. Somehow, without looking at her, Aedan knew it was the heart of Jennet. How he wanted to ease her pain!

Like little echoes, the moth-like flutters twittered and flowed excitedly—like bursts of warmth exploding inside him. A thin, dark boy twined his arm about Aedan's shoulders and sang with a piercing sweetness into his ear. Aedan glanced again at Jennet, who was wrapped about with children hugging her. There it was once more, that patient little flutter of warmth.

Light. An image came into his mind—he saw his love for Jennet as a never-ending flame, steadfast and clear, burning for all eternity. In the heart of that flame, he strove to build an image of Jennet, that she would be surrounded always by his love and care, though she would never return his feelings. A huge wave of emotion swept him. Jennet jumped, glanced around, startled.

The little flutter of warmth was repeated, like tiny impulses against his mind. Aedan grinned and squeezed the two impudent urchins who sat before him. He got the picture. This time, he built the image of a candle in his mind, then another, then a thousand tiny flames flickering in the night. These he set about Jennet as he saw her in his mind's eye. And then, satisfied, he raised his voice in song. Glancing at Jennet, he surprised a fleeting look of curiosity on her face, as though some sudden thought had caught her unawares, then she smiled to herself and tousled the hair of the little girl in her lap.

Aedan hid a small smile. Lost among the children, he could love her and not hurt her. His own tangle of pain that threatened this calm sense of victory—he would learn to live with that in good time, he hoped. For now, however, he could love her and she need never know.

Chapter 5

Enveloped in a cloak the color of gray sand, Assir slipped without a sound, almost invisible in the ebbing of the day, from building to building in the Lower City. His arm slashed in a sharp downward signal. Behind him, his father, Obal, and Barak melted into shadows.

Pacing two-by-two, a column of Corpsmen strode by. While the city of Altari-Maro was nominally free, a large body of Sindren Corpsmen was established in the Lower City. Their given purpose was to keep a watchful eye on the Empire's commercial interests, but in reality they controlled a complicated, many-tiered network of spies who came and went on—and sometimes disappeared from—the ships that plied between Altari-Maro and Western and Eastern ports.

The Empire had arisen from the long-defunct Council of Western Nations. Generations ago the entire Western world had been divided into myriad interdependent na-tions, always bickering amongst themselves and creating and breaking alliances, jockeying for supremacy in the lu-crative Eastern trade. Most of what was known about the Eastern world was based on legends and deliberate mis-information. The distances were so great that contact was limited, and since the East had never shown itself to be interested in the affairs of the Western nations, save for trade, it had stood aloof from the peripatetic shifts in political power that rippled through the West at ever shorter intervals.

Two generations ago an alliance of the great Mamut Empire with the Five Crowns of Aranth had resulted in the formation of the Council of the Western Nations. By shrewd manipulation, assassination, and sheer politicking, the Mamut Emperor had seized control of the Council—ensuring the cooperation of the member nations by holding a child of each ruler ransom for the parents'—and indeed, country's—good behavior. Children who were taught, moreover, to be Mamut puppets sent home to rule as they reached maturity. Life had not changed for most of the citizens of the Western world—the merchants and farmers and tradespeople who benefited little regardless of who sat upon which throne. All changed, however, when politics had been superseded by religion. When it became clear that the present Emperor was hand-in-glove with the Sindren Corps, 'Empire' took on a whole new meaning.

Half the known world was being drained of vitality—ideas, innovation, initiative, and identity—all were being submerged in the vicious, murky demands of the Sindren Da'a—a terrible god of wrath and consumption—a god remote, unyielding, without pity. Like a black hole, the god's priests drew in all spirit, all beauty, all that existed to gladden a soul's stay on this earth—and gave back nothing that a bewildered populace under the Corps' dominion could tell. Only those who embraced both Empire and Da'a—like Zaavan—prospered in this new world. With the might of Empire behind it, the Corps was spreading across the Western world with little effective resistance.

And when, Barak thought bitterly, the Sindren Corps was led in by such as Zaavan, resistance was smothered before it had a chance to spark.

Barak's harsh features twisted. They must find Aedan, he must not be swallowed by the dark. There must yet be a morsel of hope in this world if one bright, light-filled soul such as Aedan's could be saved. Beyond that fervent prayer, a wisp of a thought struck him. Some other idea loomed larger, deeper. He tried to concentrate, to grasp the rest of that dawning moment of awareness, then Assir beckoned them forward in the failing light. He gathered his wits together to follow Isman-Bati as his friend slipped along behind his son. Like a great shadow on the edge of night, Obal brought up the rear.

At length, Assir's slight form disappeared through a doorway, and Isman motioned Barak before him. Obal reached the doorway, grinned without humor, then froze as the merest whisper of sound reached them—like the muffled impact of a body against a wall. He drifted back into the alley with a practiced carefulness so that Isman could not see his movements. The cloth merchant signaled to someone within the warehouse. He and his companion reached Obal as he straightened over a black-robed figure slumped by a wall. The big man's eyes flared.

"A Sindren spy." He grunted and wiped his hands on his shirt as if he'd touched carrion.

Isman-Bati gestured. His companion from the warehouse stooped, slung the body over his shoulder, and made off in the direction of the waterfront. With a strong current, it could be a long time before the body was found. If ever. In that time lay safety.

The cloth merchant, a granary clerk, the jeweler's apprentice, and Shavi the harbormaster flanked Nepentha, the eldest daughter of the tailor as she took the measure of Barak and Obal. Other shadowy figures guarded the exits of the vast warehouse. Tall but not thin, Nepentha's coiled black hair was roped and caught at the nape of her neck in a silver catch. A single streak of gray swooped above one eye. Like the others, she wore a concealing cloak, now pushed back from her shoulders to reveal a peacock-blue tunic over dark trousers and rope-soled sandals. Slender, tapering fingers steepled breast-high, and, as she shifted her stance to take in the newcomers, silver-strung earrings thrummed like faint chimes from some remembered summer's eve. Thin silver bracelets shimmered at her wrists. Obal stared at her with unabashed fascination and admiration, while Barak's face revealed only his inborn alertness and caution. At last the woman drew breath to speak, her voice smoky and low, almost seductive in its cadence and tone.

"We are all children of the light in Altari-Maro. You, also, even though you do not partake of the faith. In this much, then, can we help. This boy you seek—he could not come to refuge in the City of Light unless he is wholly of the light—tutored in its mysteries or born to that knowledge."

"Then," Barak put it bluntly, "how do you explain the vision of Carrig the crystal-reader?"

Nepentha shrugged, her dark eyes glinting with ill-concealed amusement. "Perhaps he only conjured up a vision from your past, oh stalwart mountsman. Why should those of the light concern themselves with one lost boy?" Her mouth twisted. "All of the West is being plunged into darkness!"

"But his mother Anja," Obal protested, "was of the light." As Barak threw a quick, surprised glance at him, Obal shrugged. "Ilissa named her so."

Nepentha considered this.

"Half of the light? It may be that we can find some trace of him then, but," she met Barak's angry look full on, "it is certain that such as he never came alive into the City of Light."

Barak's hackles raised at the unmistakable dismissal in the woman's tone. His anger and his fear spilled into words.

"We have no need for such arrogance, my lady. Isman, I'm sorry to have put you and yours to this danger. Obal and I will leave now and search for Aedan as we may."

Obal's large hand clamped down on Barak's shoulder.

"Ho, Obal! Will you hold me now, after all these years as comrades?"

Obal's features twisted with his own despair and sorrow. He dropped his hand.

"Nay, friend. But stop up your anger and hear again this woman's words. She has said they may find some trace of the boy—mayhaps we will be given some direction in which to turn before we leave."

His unkempt brows drew down, but he met his friend's flushed face without flinching. At length Barak expelled a hissing breath and clapped Obal on the arm.

"You've spoken well, Obal. I will eat up my haste and bitterness in hopes this night will yet bear fruit—if not the harvest for which we hoped." The little man faced Is-man-Bati, all the anger drained from him and spoke from the heart, without pretense. "You have heard how it is with us, Isman-friend. Without Aedan, without the Q'tar, we will have failed his parents' trust and—."

He broke off as Isman and Nepentha exchanged a look of incredulity with their comrades, then Nepentha demanded imperiously, "What named you this boy?"

"His father gave him a decent Halfern name, after his own father it is said—Aedan," Obal explained, frowning, baffled by the sudden turn of events. Beside his bear of a friend, Barak, watchful and alert, explained further.

"Q'tar. Aedan Q'tar. His mother Anja bore him his second name."

"But, half of the light?" Nepentha half-whispered to herself. "How can this be?" Turning to Obal and Barak, she took control of the meeting again.

"Listen well. This boy, this Aedan, *must* be found. We had thought, between the few gathered here," her arms glittered as she indicated the silent group about them, "that we could scan the way for your charge and set you upon his path, but—the Q'tar!" Amazement shifted her voice a tone higher. "For this we need more time. There are others we must seek out to make contact with the City of Light."

"What goes on here?" Barak demanded. "What meaning do you take from Aedan's name?"

A slim shadow detached itself from the doorway to whisper a few words into the harbormaster's ear. Shavi touched Nepentha's sleeve.

"*They* come."

"We must go. Now." Nepentha turned to Isman-Bati. "Isman-brother, bring these two to the joining." With that, she pulled the cowl of her cloak close and disappeared into the depths of the warehouse. The others, Barak noted, melted away in separate directions even as Nepentha spoke. Isman beckoned to Assir and his friends. A ladder, which they pulled up after them, gave access to the roof. Keeping a low silhouette, the four men ran at a crouch for the adjoining roof of a neighboring warehouse. At length, they came back to ground far from the warehouse where the group had met, to make their cautious way to Isman's silent house.

A bright-eyed Bahri met them in the garden with a shielded lamp and a tray with cups of the thick hill coffee. Questions struggled across her young face, but she left them unasked as her older brother took the tray from her as they left their father with his friends. Eying Isman's self-composed profile, Barak schooled himself to patience, drank his coffee, and waited for the man to speak. The cloth merchant raised his eyes after a long moment and met the gazes of Obal and Barak.

"The name 'Q'tar' is known to the people of the light. In times of great need, my friends, the Q'tar has come forth to serve as a focal point for the power of the light. Like a funnel, the Q'tar channels the light to push back the dark."

"How is this 'Q'tar chosen?" Obal put the wary question to his friend.

""They are known at birth," Isman explained, "because they hold no light, but are not of the dark. He shrugged as Barak started to speak, then seemed to think better of whatever he meant to say. "The Q'tar reflects all goodness, yet hoards none—giving back the light. They are innocent, empty, ready to take the light."

"How," Barak chose his words with care, his unspoken fear rough in his voice, "if they come too close to the power of the light with none of their own?"

Isman heaved a deep sigh.

"The Q'tar must come willingly, Barak-friend, for many have died serving as such when the need was great."

"You name yourself friend," Obal's low growl rumbled with pain, "yet you would seek young Aedan for a near-certain death? To what avail would his life be against the dark god's spawn—the Sindren?"

Isman sat without flinching.

"The Q'tar is like a prism, Obal—a beautifully faceted, clear stone. Alone it is harmless, yet let the light pass through such and one may find a spark leaping to flame. Death is a risk, but that spark may burn the Western world free of the dead god Da'a and his sack-faced followers. The very soul of the West is being shriven away. How much more can we take until we all surrender or die?

"Aedan has a choice," Isman stated flatly. "The Light does not take unwilling victims."

The gray shroud of early morning fluttered about the edges of the night's dispersal. The great mound that was Obal stirred, groaned, stirred again. Rubbing his eyes with the ball of his thumb, he addressed his friend in a hoarse whisper.

"Day breaks, Barak. Have you decided whether to stay or go hence on our own?"

The pallid light brooded shadows across Barak's thin browned features, deepening the hollows left from a sleepless night. Most of it had been spent pacing the floor between his bed and Obal's. Now he sank onto his bed and faced Obal, his dark eyes wide, his voice low.

"How can we take our leave, Obal, as ignorant of his whereabouts as when we came? Needs must, I think, stay."

"Aye," Obal concurred. "At least until we can find out more of this joining."

"As to the rest—" Barak shook his head without finishing.

"He must be told," Obal insisted, "for he is his parents' son and must take his own counsel." He shifted his weight, pulling his blanket closer against the dead morning chill. "Sleep now, little dagger. The lad is not a fool to rush in without a thought. We've always trusted him in the past to know what's best."

"If we find him before *they* do." He did not need to name who *they* were. The Sindren Corps. For it seemed to Barak, that now they could understand why Zaavan had sent men to hunt down the son who had been no more than the heir of a minor Halfern holding. He lay down and pulled his blanket close against that cold thought.

In two's, three's and singly, figures slipped into the great marshy hollow which Obal and Barak had overlooked so many years before. All came without speaking and assumed their place within a ring three-persons deep until perhaps a hundred or more had gathered. Isman-Bati and Mari-Isman stood beside the two outsiders beyond the rings. When the rings were complete, a small group made its way into the heart of the circle, linked each to each, facing outward. Barak recognized Nepentha's tall form as she raised her hand in the center of the circle. The rings parted before her, creating a pathway to where Barak and Obal waited with their friends. The cloth merchant and his weaver wife nudged them forward until they too stood enclosed at the center of the rings.

Nepentha brought her hands out of the folds of her robe. The candle that she held sprang to light as she raised her cowled head. Beside them and all around them, one by one, candles flickered to life. Even as the prism had foretold, the hooded figures tightened the circle as Isman and Mari-Isman lit two candles from their own and handed the tiny, glowing lights to Obal and to Barak.

"Look into the heart of the light," Nepentha's smoky voice commanded, "and your eyes shall discover your young charge, Aedan, if he is yet to be found on this earth. Seek ye the spirit of lightness, for the Q'tar is pure, unfettered by the dark."

No sound raked the broken edge of night, save for his own heartbeat, it seemed to Barak. The golden, leaping flame before him flared with a compelling brightness, higher, swelling until he saw only the light. Outside the light, it seemed to him that he could feel the joining of those others nearby to his quest, and yet even farther away, as if presences from great distances were also enjoined in their effort. A vast, searching light illumined his memories of Aedan and those of Obal to send a probing beam into the night. His eyes straining, Barak sought to hold that joining.

Aedan, astride a fat-flanked pony, solemn eyes flaring with delight as his chubby knees nudged and the pony trotted off obediently... Aedan deftly kicking a ducchi ball past a gaggle of the holding's children... Aedan's face lost in weary respite, the fever beading across his forehead....

Those remembered moments moved closer and closer to the present. In the hollow, the intensity of the search mounted, until Barak's mind seemed to implode from the effort. Now images swept across his mind of clear water coursing down white rapids in high mountains. As if viewed from an eagle's flight, a clumsy boat tooled along the river—a toy that moved slowly but steadily between the mountains. The eagle might have been plummeting down, down towards the rocky, winding riverbed, for the boat grew larger, larger, filling their minds. A black canvas shelter loomed in the center of the craft, held by intricate lashing to wooden posts in a repeating twined pattern—not of rope, but of some pliable, sinuous plant. Beyond the shelter, the back of a small, dark man bent to a pole. Not Aedan! Barak fairly screamed with impatience. Within the shelter?

A sudden shudder rippled through the ranks of those joined in the hollow. The images slurred, skewed, fragmented and were lost, only to be replaced by a wide-eyed slender young woman with deep hollows beneath her eyes—eyes that stared with twin flames of astonishment into those of Barak and the company about him. His eyes shot open as harsh swearing marked Obal beside him.

"Mother of Light! How came this girl to break our hold?"

A muffled shout arrested any reply Barak might have made.

"The Corps! To safety!"

Lights blinked out and figures cut and ran from the ranks in all directions. Obal stood his ground, staying Isman and Mari with a large hand. Barak waited.

"Take cover, my friends. Let's find out which quarter the wind is in before we run with the herd."

Half sunken in the marshy edges of the hollow, surrounded by thick clumps of tall, green-jointed reeds, Barak parted a thick fistful with a stealthy hand to view the emptied hollow. From the north edge, away from the city, poured a stream of riders. Nowhere was there the slightest movement or sound from the dispersal of the gathering, but Barak could feel other eyes, like his own, peering into that night, calculating the chances of making it back to the city past that mounted cohort. The leader gestured and the riders fanned out.

Barak thought about his companions with a grim determination. If his friends could make it back to the city, the hunt for Aedan would continue. Those mounted Corpsmen would be carrying lieber-sabers. They could and would cut down anything or anyone started into their path. The only hope for his friends was to create a diversion to draw the riders in one direction, giving some of their party a chance to escape. Pushing all thought, all hope of Aedan from his mind, Barak signaled his intent to Obal. How often in the past had they faced some danger just like this?

Taking care to conceal his movements as best he could, sweat soaking the small of his back, Barak circled about to the left while Obal moved to their right. Isman and Mari were already drifting half-submerged in the swampy water of the marsh, moving away from the hollow as fast as they dared. Barak counted to fifteen, then lobbed a handful of pebbles in all directions. Like an echo, similar sounds and shaking of reeds rippled out from his position. The same idea must have occurred to others among their compatriots in the gathering. The Corpsmen checked their sweep, hesitating as their leader pointed first in Barak's direction, then opposite. Their second's hesitation cost them,. For another shower of pebbles set their mounts to prancing. A furious shout from the leader scattered the riders into the reeds in all directions, sabers drawn.

Like a melting shadow, Barak changed direction and attempted to put some distance between himself and his former position. In the ensuing melee, lieber-sabers slashed at the air, scything reeds. Barak winced in a sudden arc of light. That one had caught a fugitive who screamed in agony before slumping half-charred onto a marshy tuft of grass. No hope for that one! Here the horses had slowed their forward rush into the swamp, some of the Corpsmen dismounting to comb the reeds on foot. A rider came close to Barak's hiding place. In one quick movement, the Corpsman was pulled from his mount, a blade slipped in one practiced motion into place, and the body dropped into the muck. Barak slapped the horse on the flank, sending it leaping back towards the other riders.

A great bellow assaulted the air. Obal! Checking his stealthy, forward movement, Barak peered into the roiling boil of riders crisscrossing the hollow. Were those hooded Corpsmen dragging someone before their leader? For one Corpsman, flanked by two other riders, had not entered the fray. Straining to see, Barak shifted his position into the night air. Whoever those black monks held, their prisoner yet lived to struggle. If only he could get closer! Dropping back into the shelter of the reeds, he froze. There was movement to his right. A sharp green light rent the air before him, dazzling his night sight. A second burst grazed his temple as he threw himself to the ground. The world exploded into a multi-hued shower of lights before the ground rose up to meet him and conscious thought broke.

By morning's pale light, five prisoners were led or carried like limp sacks of waterlogged goods into the Sindren Corps' compound on the verge of the Upper City. In the stir of early market sellers and stall-owners, Obal pulled his hood free and bent to the raising of Isman's cart to the horse's traces. That sagging bundle he marked well. Beside him, Assir's deft hands steadied the horse as he flicked a warning glance at his towering companion.

With a helpless fury coursing through him, Obal watched as the gates swung shut behind the last Corpsman. As he followed the slow pace of the cart to the wharf, his untidy brows furrowed in despair. Had that truly been Barak—trussed like a gangli-hen for roasting? Aedan—lost to them still! His great heart ached and he longed to throw back his head and howl with the pain that built inside him. And that woman! If ever he lay hands on her! What knew she of his lost charge? He would have the answer from her, himself, with his bare hands, if ever he came across her. Unclenching his massive fists, he met Assir's worried gaze with more control than he felt. Now they knew. Barak could have survived the night's tumultuous ending. First to find a way to free the little man and his four companions, then they could be off to seek Aedan once more. And, if they should come too late to Barak—or to Aedan, for that matter, he swore a silent vow to himself, he would spend the rest of his days seeking the woman who had interrupted their quest. She would forfeit her life for her actions that night!

Chapter 6

Driftless and dreamless, Jennet sat in the garden and watched the music rippling from the paraqwet's throat. The tiny bird's chest rose and fell in a pulsating flash of crimson and green. The world was reduced for her to light and color and a collage of evermore changing, shifting images. She saw the faces of Patar Q'an and the Lady and the youth who swept the staircase, the old woman who sold only yellow lin-lin posies in the market, the grinning cheerful trooping of children on their way to morning classes. Out of their mouths wove patterns of light, bemusing and delighting her.

Now she felt herself flowing into the light, images rising to greet her beyond the City of Light. She saw tiny villages tucked into forest clearings, large cities perched and dazzling on hillsides, solitary figures tending fields, people like pinpoints of color transporting across space and time. She was aware that she could see these and know them for individual travelers, but that she herself was on some higher path of consciousness. She was free of her unwilling bond, free to explore the teachings of the City—the wild, undisciplined yearnings that had plagued her childhood at last to have pattern, order, and control.

Minutes passed and the focus of the panorama of images shifted. The world beneath her with its multi-colored levels of reality and consciousness grew more remote. Even her identity, it seemed to her, was submerging, melting, becoming diffused into some vast canopy of contentment. How long she sat thus, she could not tell. At some point, weighty and drowsy with this merging, she began to withdraw herself from the flow, skein by skein unraveling that which was Jennet from the whole.

Withdrawal was different, something had changed. As she drew in those strands of herself, they uncurled from and touched other strands and with each of these contacts, a wave of interest and concern joined with her, so that strand by strand the laborious careful untangling of her mind moved faster and faster. She read joy and sadness and curiosity in those sparks between herself and those others.

Altogether herself again, she began to withdraw her consciousness one level at a time, coming closer and closer to that real world, where some stirring of hunger or pain in her body had set up that recall. She understood as she descended, though, that by conscious will and act, she could leave the earthbound, physical part of her being behind and climb one last time to that high, serene blending of awareness and remain forever entwined there.

Even as those thoughts formed, she was aware, too, that she did not hesitate, but moved with unerring intention and with certainty down and down that spiral of consciousness. Close now, she looked once again upon the world below her—upon the enormous, restless oceans sprawling against the coasts of continents, and closer yet, upon the verdant iridescent sparkling of the vast concealing rainforest that held the City of Light. Closer, here were the blue and green and yellow haze of thought and emotion of ordinary peoples.

And here, too, she noticed pulsating black fingers thick in the West. Where these reached, encircling all other areas, all color, all harmony disappeared. It was as if some miasmic disease spread, choking all life where it took hold. There, where the mountains in which she'd been born thrust to the sky, not a flicker of thought permeated the denseness of that spreading plague. Elsewhere, those black pulses were fainter, or retreated and advanced in erratic patterns.

Skimming towards Abri-Hataro, Jennet was sickened. Here, all was green and life-affirming. The Sindren Corps had not breached the defenses of the city, but she could see with a nauseating clarity the inevitable growth of that black blight until their world hung drifting in space, weighted and cold. What could she do to stop it? Better surely to make her choice and withdraw now to the eternal safety and security she had just shared.

Indecisive, she hesitated, pleading, whirling about—one color among many. And was met by silence. She knew, how well she knew it, that she alone could take responsibility for herself, choose to go forward or take that last irreversible step back. 'Look, then,' she admonished herself, 'at these others.' For long moments, her panic controlled, Jennet gazed into the patterns of color woven all about her and tried to see her way clear.

There—something insistent drew her mind's eye. That singular strand she recognized as herself—winding and random—not in the present, but like a trail of light written on the past, fading even as she tried to follow it. With fierce concentration, she focused on that trail. Fainter, then brighter it wound. But, there! See how it touched, holding to a thread even more diffuse and convoluted than her own. See how that contact sustained, gathered up that other life, and together they moved like an arrow—two strands always—through time, arching in a shower of light into the City of Light.

With a jolt, Jennet opened her eyes upon starlight, seeing not the paraqwet before her—long stilled, sleeping among the blooming branches of the yousli tree—but those two strands of life, purpose meshed, moving as one yet remaining two distinct threads at all times. Hands to her face, the bitter silent sobs shook her. Aedan had gone, and she had let him go without a farewell, without a word of encouragement or concern or care. He had faced himself and with a steadfastness of purpose had rejected Abri-Hataro—its security and enticements shed as easily as childhood treats. He'd spoken to the Lady of friends and holding and a debt to parents now dead. She'd barely heard, dismissing him as provincial and afraid, while she planned to take up the pursuit of greater knowledge, truth, and beauty. She remembered now, how the Lady had accepted his decision, blessed him, and sent him on his way herself when he had rejected the offer of Patar to accompany him.

Stretching, she straightened her cramped limbs and made her way to her room, moving as stiff as an arthritic elder. Moonlight poured in at the window, throwing a bright sweep of light into the bedroom, its furnishings in shadow. A spasm of doubt shook her resolve—this small spare room signified her acceptance, her acknowledged membership in the community of Abri-Hataro. How could she walk away from it? Yet, she crossed to a low woven chest beside her bed and opened it. In a matter of minutes her packing was complete; the lightweight bundle in her hands declared her intentions.

A mind-numbing weariness engulfed her. Sleep—she must force herself to lie down and rest until the dawn's first graying eased the night's slow grip on time. With morning she would speak to the Lady, then she too would turn her back on the City of Light. How or when she would find Aedan, whether or not he would accept her aid, whether in fact she could be of any use to him in his struggle—these were questions that only time could resolve. Jennet lay down on her bed and closed her eyes, as if to shut away those persistent, harrying worries. Bit by bit, her mind quieted and as she drowsed, a curious, comforting image overtook her. A thousand flickering lights surrounded her, enveloping her with peace so that she might at last relax and give in to sleep.

Aedan walked along the shore trail, leading the ponies, keeping a wary eye behind and before him. The Lady had set him back at the falls' edge. The sight of Jennet's mount cost him a moment's fierce doubt when he'd stared back into the mists of the rushing waterfall and wondered if he were making the right choice in passing up the chance to stay close to Jennet. Better, it seemed to him in that moment's regretful longing, to have stayed. In time perhaps she would have come to love him—or to acknowledge to them both that she did love. What was the use? He turned back to the patient, nodding ponies. She had already made her choice clear, and he—well, his future was not entirely in his own hands. What had his old tutor Dostven said? That from the moment of his birth, his *m'airi* had been shaped—was even now being shaped—by the world in which he lived.

And that, he thought, was the crux of the matter. He did not belong in the City of Light. He was a son of the holding, and like his father before him that was the core of his world, wherever he might wander, to whatever field of endeavor he might put his mind and hands. Someday he would return to the holding.

With renewed resolution, then, he stowed his renewed provisions in Dobbet's saddlebags, mounted Bracken, and set off along the riverbank where the going was easier. For nearly a week, by his careful reckoning, he traveled thus, camping each night—meeting no one, finding no sign of a human presence anywhere in the vast forests about him. Three days ago the high valley had narrowed to a gap in the encircling mountains. A precipitous drop greeted him, forcing him to sidetrack into the forest to search out a way down. At last, he came out within a lower valley. Making his way back to the river, he came upon the unmistakable signs of human intrusion—a faint trail that, after a day's travel, became more noticeable. Where it would lead him, or to whom, he could not foresee.

Now, however, the trail widened out beyond where he stopped to the river's bank. Standing concealed above the trail's final downward curve, he saw pilings at measured intervals running out into the deeper waters of the river. No huts, no boats, no human activity stirred in the still morning sun. No evidence of human presence was apparent save for the presence of those pilings. Aedan's apprehensive, roving gaze skirted the clearing, faltered. He could move unseen around the edges of the clearing, but of the path, there was no sign on the other side of the clearing. It ended here at the river. Or, his eyes narrowed, began here.

Making up his mind, he led the ponies into the forest above the clearing, hobbled both that they might graze, and settled himself in comfort under the shade of the trees, where he could watch the landing below. The sun advanced across the sky above him, marking the somnolent progression of the day. The forest was silent behind him. Even the ponies appeared to sleep in the shade. Below, the river lapped in lazy waves at the shore. Aedan shook himself free of his lethargy, made a rough lunch of bread and fruit, drank deeply from his water bag, and then settled down to watch again. This time he could not fight the heat, the torpor that crept over his mind.

Seek ye the Boatman, plying the river,
For thy path, high-born, leads to the sea.
Step down to the shore and pay thy fare.
Then shall the molten river guide thee
Succor thee, aid thee! This is the third
Observation of the Quoran Dru.

Aedan's eyes opened. Shadows now slanted from the path of an afternoon sun. The scene below remained unchanged. He rose, stretched, drank again, and then freed the wide-eyed ponies that watched him with gentle, uncurious eyes. A bird's startled cry rang out as he breeched the forest and made his way into the clearing.

Once there, he led the ponies to the water's edge, where they drank their fill. Securing their reins to a small bush beneath the lush canopy of an overhanging zydr tree, he went back to the river and waded in. The water was cool and refreshing after the enclosed heat of the forest above. Lying back, he floated for a while, then turned and swam to the nearest piling. One line of them stood sentinel—moving straight out into the river bed. They might have been hewn of the wood of the zydr itself, so massive and ancient were the pilings. The current, he noted, was stronger away from the shore. Thinking on this, he turned and swam back to shallower waters.

Hanging in the water, his quick gaze sought the ponies. Reassured by their undisturbed placidity, his gaze wandered across the shoreline. The play of light and shadow intrigued him. Then he straightened, looked from the pilings to the shore, squinting as he calculated. Regaining

the shore with a few powerful strokes, he shook himself
and inspected the bank. The high water marks were clear
now that he recognized them for what they were. And,
he judged, recent. High enough—his gaze swept the river
again—to cover those pilings. The wood above water was
as dark and wet as that below.

When would the river flood again, rendering the landing hidden from prying eyes? How was it that now, when
he'd come to the end of the trail, the beach was clear?
He shook his head in his impatience. He was losing time
watching an empty cove. There was no boatman, nor even
a boat here. Time he gathered up his gear and took his
chances on picking up the trail again on the far side of the
forest. Yet, he did not move, but closed his eyes.

Half-a-child of the light, he could not disappear like
Jennet, and he could not summon the light. But he could
feel it all around him—flowing into him, warming him
heart and soul. *'Have faith,'* he told himself and held that
thought. When he opened his eyes, a flat boat was nosing
along the piers, poled fore and aft by two small, dark men.
How? They moved the craft in with a swiftness that spoke
of long familiarity, tying it to the last pilings and cranking down a ramp that bit into the soft sand at the water's
edge.

"'E be daft, 'e be." The forward poler was ebony-dark,
his gray hair grizzled and close-cropped. Wiry and honed
by hard work, his muscles rippled as he made the craft
fast. It was only when he spoke again that Aedan belat-
edly understood the old man was speaking of him.

"'Ere, ye daft boy, bring along them animals. Step lively, step lively! Watcher be thinking of, a'keeping the Boatman waiting! See now, river's rising, river's rising."

The old man nodded vigorously and Aedan, galvanized into action, saw that the water level was rising. Jumping into action, he retrieved Dobbet and Bracken. They mounted the ferry ramp without a misstep, the old man cranking up the ramp and casting off as soon as the animals were clear. Steadily, they moved back into the current of the river, waves lapping high on the sides of the river barge. Even as they moved downriver, the deep waters bit at the exposed, forlorn beach, until, looking back, Aedan could no longer tell where he'd come aboard—pilings and beach both hidden.

"Aye, Eben," the elderly black man raised his gruff voice to the silent young man behind him, "'ave a care, keep 'er steady." He pulled in and fastened his own pole, gesturing at Aedan.

"Why 'e be a'standing like a statue in the rain? Move, ye dimwitted child of the light and get them ponies under cover."

Aedan started, turned. In the center of the barge stood a shelter, a black canvas contraption open on one side, secured to pliant wood and lashed about in a complicated, fine pattern of entwined vines, some of which still bore green leaves. The old man shooed his charge before him like a gangli-hen with a wayward chick. Within the shelter, a rail ran before a makeshift feed box filled with grain. Aedan had no trouble urging his mounts into the sheltered space. To his left, the wide space sported several hammocks now drawn up out of the way, vine-covered bins holding an array of foodstuffs, rope, clothing, huge orange gourds, a live bird that watched Aedan with un-blinking dark eyes, and various and sundry odds and ends.

The old man pulled down the nearest hammock and secured it.

"'Ere be, boy, stow yer gear quick now." Aedan did as he was bid, and then the grizzled fellow pointed aft with his chin. "Sit ye down out of the way, boy. Time it 'tis to get this 'ere boat a'moving downriver."

"Please, sir," Aedan found his voice at last as he obeyed, sitting sideways onto the swaying hammock. "Where are we going?"

The small man rolled dark eyes skyward and shook his head in reproof.

"I be the Boatman, boy, and we be riding the river till she stops. Now leave me be. This 'ere boat don't steer it-self."

From behind the shelter came a husky sigh, then a deep serene voice lifted in song. Aedan could not under-stand the words, but the melody and rhythm sank into his bones, rooted in the bitter longing of his heart. It eased that soreness he felt at parting from Jennet even as he tried to settle himself more comfortably in the hammock and stared out at the bank that was moving with surpris-ing speed past his range of sight.

Chapter 7

The Abri-Corazon was still in the first soft wash of dawn as Jennet hefted her pack, gave a last regretful look about her room, then padded down the wide stairs. Bakti, the cat, ignored her and swarmed up a trellised lin-lin vine, emerging from the opening sweep of white blossoms to leap in a long, lean stretch from the trellis to the hall. Settling itself in the sun, the cat turned its back on Jennet and began to wash its face. She could hear it purring from where she stood. Walking into the Great Hall, she headed at a brisk pace across the vast colonnaded space to an obscure door set in the far corner beyond the dais. Leaving her pack beside the door, she opened it onto a screened portico which looked out upon a tiny, tranquil garden. Here, too, even at this early hour, the Lady sat like a statue—the lids of her eyes seemed heavy as stone, rolled with age and weighted with a burden not entirely banished by the beauty of the light's first coming into day. Jennet checked, hesitant to disturb the ancient one's peace.

"Enter, child-Jennet."

Jennet crossed to stand before her, feeling like a penitent come before a priest, but the Lady's steady gray eyes met her own with an overwhelming serenity. A gnarled hand reached out to draw the young woman to her side. Giving Jennet a swift, shrewd glance, the Lady eyed the marks of the restless night that haunted the edges of youth in the face before her.

"You will follow the Q'tar." At Jennet's nervous nod, the Lady continued. "The City of Light opens its arms to its children, my Jennet. Do not believe that its love cannot go with you when you are no longer within the Abri-Corazon.

"You must not berate yourself for a false pride, for a choice made in haste. Even as the Q'tar must answer to his own *m'airi*, yours comes no more easily, no more clearly than for any other child of the light." A wry tone warmed her voice. "Even I, child-Jennet, have in a long and varied life not always seen eye-to-eye with the demands of time, have wished to surrender to my own desire to retreat from this physical world." Her voice lifted and she clasped Jennet's hand between her own. "But it was not meant to be, not for me. Nor for you—not yet, it seems."

Jennet blushed and lifted her face to meet the Lady's gaze.

"I've been a fool, my Lady. And yet, how could I tell between them—the false tie and that which grew out of ordinary respect and liking?" She would not, even to the Lady, admit that other, more wounding pride that had made her deny and try to kill her love. That love—itself a product of the Light—she checked her own silent recriminations. Time, later, to deal with that mistake—if it were not already too late.

The Lady gathered her loose gray robes about her and stood, pulling Jennet up with her. They paced towards an open door behind the garden.

"You must have a care, Jennet," the old woman stated, then paused, "for this Q'tar...." Her voice trailed off as if she were lost in her thoughts, then she turned her gaze on Jennet.

"This Q'tar, if he lives, may surprise us all. You, Jennet," she chuckled softly, "may surprise yourself."

"My Lady?"

The ancient one gave no indication that she heard that startled query, but stepped through the doorway and loosed her hold on Jennet's arm. Dilys' robes rustled in the clear, quiet air as she came to meet her lady. The old woman turned. Jennet dropped to one knee and kissed the hand of blessing the Lady extended to her. Returning quickly through the garden to retrieve her light pack, she made her way into the Great Hall, looking about with a sharp jerk of her head as a shadow melted from the wall to join her.

Patar Q'an held out his hands, a pack much like her own strapped to his back over his cloak.

"Come, Jennet! Let us make our way into the Light, now, as it rises to greet us."

Riding the light with Patar Q'an's strength to guide her, Jennet and her companion came out of the light onto the forested flanks of a low rounded, remnant of a volcanic core. The sun tilted towards afternoon as they strode downslope, Patar Q'an setting a pace that left little breath, nor yet, attention, to question their present whereabouts—much less their immediate destination. At length, his pace slowed and he flopped belly-down to drink from the sparkling pool of the tiny stream they'd been following downhill. Jennet dropped her pack and with haste mimicked the older man's example, afraid he'd be up and off again before she quenched her thirst. He straightened up, grunted, and dropped his pack on the ground. Stretching his shoulders, Patar Q'an settled against the bole of a young zydr tree. Drawing hard bread and cheese from his pack, he tossed a good-sized chunk of bread her way and grinned.

"Eat, Jennet."

Ravenous, Jennet didn't need to force herself to finish both bread and cheese, drinking her fill from the stream once again after she'd eaten. She filled her canteen before she faced her companion. Patar Q'an seemed bemused by the sweet trilling of some unseen bird.

"Patar," she began, "why have you come? Where do we go now? Aedan," her voice tripped over his name, "Aedan does not wait below."

That, at least, was not a question. Wherever he went now, it was not here. Such was her fever of impatience, her self-chastisement, she would have known instantly if he were within reach.

Patar waited until the bird's sweet song was eclipsed by silence before answering in a soft voice.

"Your quest is also mine, sweet Jennet. The Q'tar may help those of the light turn back the rising tide of dark." His eyes bore into hers with a pain that went far deeper than mere hatred or religious fervor. "There is a soul that hangs in the balance, Jennet. She must be set free!"

Horrified understanding broke and she remembered, too late, the fate of Patar's wife. Then he shrugged, damping back the load of grief he carried.

"As to where we go, my child, why down to the village. Santiagar lies on the northern shore of Biscal Island." He caught Jennet's start of recognition and nodded. "Yes, child. We have come to light in the Sindalar Islands. Why here?" He forestalled her next question and gestured at the forest about them. "Because here we will pick a load of chama leaves and take them down to the house of a man I know in Santiagar. Biscal is known for its chama harvest. The leaves will fetch a good price, and," his grin bared even white teeth, "provide us with a reason for appearing at the house of Inlan-Chu.

"Inlan-Chu," he explained, "is a son of the light. He is also a station on the path of the light."

"Then," Jennet interrupted with an eagerness she could not hide, "he can show us where to find Aedan! Yes?"

Patar Q'an stood and shrugged his arms into the straps of his pack once more. He extended a hand to Jennet as she rose.

"We who serve the Q'tar, Jennet, may find our path winding and obscure. Help may be rendered from a distance as well as at his side. There are those who must protect and those who serve best by distraction and deception, who link together pockets of dissent against the darkness by spreading hope like light."

Setting off down the hill once more, Patar Q'an left Jennet standing open-mouthed behind him. That she would not come directly to Aedan! The bitter thought worried at her, but after a near stumble, she put her mind to the task before her with a grim determination.

The soft rumble of Inlan-Chu's and Patar's voices glossed over the tiny rustlings of leaves and small night creatures as Jennet paced slowly in Inlan Chu's secluded garden. The moon was even now clearing the crest of the low slopes that crowded Santiagar onto the very shore of the island. The faint, sweet smell of chama leaves clung to her clothes. As Patar had promised, they'd picked a fair quantity of the fragrant, broad leaves, securing them in their cloaks. The leaves, when crushed, were used in a poultice that fought infection, and when brewed, made a tea that aided the healing of blistered, red throats—a common childhood ailment. Nearing Santiagar, the pair had encountered others—singly or in small groups of twos or threes—who'd been harvesting the bounty of the forest in meat or fruits or herbs, on their way to homes in the village.

Inlan-Chu, an elderly widower who lived in a comfortable villa on the edge of town, had shown no surprise at their coming, but welcomed Patar like a sorely-missed friend. The two men's talk was full of old times and acquaintances, much to Jennet's simmering impatience. Now, after dinner, they were discussing news of the northern mainland and the Mamut Empire. Fidgeting in her seat as the two men drank cups of the strong island coffee, Jennet excused herself for a walk in the garden.

Would they never turn to the reason for their visit? What did she care about the fortunes of Empire? Then she halted, sank onto a bench, and composed her raging thoughts. By the Light! Child, Patar called her, and like a child she was acting. She forced herself to face her companion's earlier statement. If she must help Aedan from a distance, then it would behoove her to pay attention. Patar was no fool. Reviewing the conversation that had taken them through dinner, she realized the common thread of the news Inlan-Chu had imparted. The Mamut Empire was having trouble up and down the length and breadth of the Naransai Mountains. Tax revenues had been burnt in the fields of the northern plains and ships with full cargoes had set sail from southern ports never to reach their intended harbors. It seemed, she puzzled it out one step at a time, that everywhere within the former Five Crowns of Aranth pockets of active resistance existed. A shudder went through her and she resumed her pacing.

The Sindren Corps was equally active and reprisals were swift—not in the name of the Empire, but in the name of Da'a. Blame for the sporadic acts of defiance was placed on demons and dragons called to earth by pagan defilers of the Dark God. Those held responsible for calling the blasphemous forces were drawn and quartered by lieber-saber in the squares of the nearest small towns and villages. Yet, such reprisals prompted new acts of covert rebellion. Nets were cut on Sindren fisher-fleets, trees felled across temple thoroughfares, and fences pulled down from temple-held pastures.

These random acts continued. Common ordinary people fought back as best they could. Random! What if, the sudden thought came to Jennet, what if word spread among the villages and towns, from ship to ship, harbor to town, mountains to plains, that the Q'tar was found and moving amongst them? Then would hope spread like wildfire, then would an organized resistance to Empire and Sindren Corps be possible. Then, too, perhaps the once-alliance could be drawn into the fray.

Jennet's gaze sought the full moon glowing like a bright beacon in this southern sky. She would be that guide, that whisper of hope. She would travel until her life gave out, if need be, to draw out the faint, precarious threads of light that pulsed throughout the Western world. But, as her gaze lingered on the moon, she thought, let her heart seek what solace it could find in this moment. Where did Aedan rest this night? Had he come yet to those friends who had drawn him from the City of Light? Her sight drifted, focused inward, and she found herself chanting the song of seeking, letting the love she held within her heart channel her wish that Aedan be safe this night.

It seemed to her that her song was swelling, as if a thousand upraised voices joined in her seeking. And in that moment, that inner light flickered, waned about the edges, was encircled. She stood outside herself, as if her mind divided and one part sang those yearning, graceful notes of seeking, spilling them into a well of light whose source came not from Jennet. Yet, around this well, shadows advanced. Somewhere, someone else sought Aedan. And beyond that seeking!

Jennet sent an urgent warning, a cry of frustration into the heart of that circle of light. A pair of dark eyes met her own, opened wide in astonishment. A man swore. She had a fleeting impression of a circle of light, figures shadowed at its center, before the light rippled and she knew her warning came too late. The forces of darkness were at hand. A great bellow shook her tenuous contact. All light, all thought broke, and she stared at a benign moon shining above Inlan-Chu's garden. Shaken, Jennet shivered in the breeze. Patar must be told. One thought sustained her, small comfort that it was. Aedan might come too late to his friends, but that he had not been among those in that circle of light, she was absolutely certain. Wherever he might find himself this night, by the Light, he was safe. He must be.

Chapter 8

Aedan lay in his hammock and slept. He dropped into a deep sleep and dreamed the dream of the dragon again. The dragon-legends had entranced many a young child, and he had often dreamed of them as a young boy. Dragons, according to legend, rode the light and slept on a golden hoard, bathed by light even in the midst of darkness. And when the fierce old dragons or their young awoke—high before the sun they flew to draw in the savage power of the light and spew it forth in a terrible scourge of fire against the forces of the dark.

Her face came in such dreams. A dim remembrance of a sweet face in its glory of dark curls. *Mother.* What stories she had told him. How the first children of the light befriended the dragons and rode them against the wind. How a dragon would sing for its brother, deep in a lair. '*I want to ride a dragon, Mother!*' he would say to her and she would tousle his hair and snuggle him closer, and reply with a soft laugh against his cheek, '*One day, little dragon-brother, you will ride the wind.*'

The soft sizzle and hissing of steam woke Aedan from his dreams. A dragon? He lay in his hammock, wondering if his senses had been deceived by his dreams, when a ball of fire cleared the trees on the far bank, arching high against the night sky before plummeting into the black-glassed smoothness of the river with another hiss and sizzle at contact. A flurry of fireballs flared and popped. Extricating himself from the unfamiliar hammock, Aedan made his way outside the shelter and found the Boatman there before him. None of the mysterious flares, he noted with relief and quick interest, struck anywhere near their anchorage.

"What?" He began, but the old man held up a hand. Aedan waited in growing annoyance. Where was the boat going? Why was he on it? What mischief was this that had awakened him in the middle of the night? Several moments elapsed; no other balls came flaming into the river. A small, impatient sound escaped him. The Boatman turned about, his grizzled features barely visible in the dim starlight, for this night wore no bright moonshine.

"They be a marker, boy, and a calling. Heed the calling well, boy."

"Eben," he raised his singsong voice and a sleepy mumble responded. "Eben, it's time." He put out a hand to Aedan's shoulder and thrust him in the direction of the shelter. "Out o' the way, boy, out o' the way. Get ye inside and prepare for the calling and the response."

"But," Aedan sputtered, and stood his ground. Why couldn't he get a straight answer from this man? "What is the calling, Boatman, and what has it to do with me?"

The old man heaved a deep sigh and shook his head.

"Boy, ye be always asking, always asking. Have ye no eyes to see with, no ears to hear with? The light, boy, the light.

"The river will flame with the light in the heart of darkness. Boat can't go on land, must go on the river. Can't go back, must go for'ard."

And, indeed, Aedan felt the slight shudder of the craft as the anchor came up and Eben shifted it into the current. Even as he felt that first tremor in the boards beneath his feet, the river before them sprang to flame. A solid line of fire, like an eerie weir, covered the river not more than a hundred yards ahead. And he the fish to be caught? Aedan turned as bidden to return to the shelter, hesitated, gripped the rail and stood his ground. The wall of flame cut across the river in an all-enveloping inferno. The ferryboat flowed toward it, the Boatman and Eben like fixed ebony pillars, grimacing with a ferocious concentration and impervious to his shouts of warning.

Once before he had faced certain death. Then his *m'airi* had been for life, and Jennet had brought him to safety. Another scene flashed through his thoughts, as he recalled that wild leap from the falls in Jennet's wake. This time the tie between them was broken. Jennet would not rescue him. A chilling futility swept over him. His hand dropped from the metal warmed at his waist. A dagger would not save him from the fire.

He closed his eyes, his thoughts confused. What of his mother and father, both dead before him? How had they met their ends? Embraced death as a welcome release or railed against its untimely appearance? He raised a hand as if to ward off the inevitable approach of the fire, then his lips moved and he heard a voice cold with terror chanting in the night.

Thrust thy hand into the heart of the flame,
High-born, to sear the sharp wind borne of fear
Into a stillness as absolute as faith.
Give thyself unto the fire—then shalt
Thou stride forth unharmed. This is the fourth
Observation of the Quoran Dru.

He recognized his own strained voice, hoarse with fear, followed by those of the Boatman and Eben, raised in some song he did not understand. The ferryboat sailed into the flames.

Slap. Slap. Slap. The regularity of that monotonous tempo roused Aedan from a stupor in which he had lost himself and all awareness of the outside world in the intricate lashings of the shelter above him. The black twine curled and wove in and out, creating bas-relief patterns of nested figure-eights and spirals that held the shelter taut against wind and storm. The roof too was woven, with mat after mat equally intricate, interlocked in a secure waterproof covering. How many hours, now, had he spent swaying in this hammock while an unknown Boatman guided him who knew where?

That thought sent a tiny, rippling question along his nerve ends. His gaze shifted down to his body and he saw his arms folded neatly across his blanketed chest. Another infinitesimal shifting of his eyes. Daylight flooded the shelter—a cool gray light with a hint of chill—like autumn crisping after a late Halfern summer. And that sound—as if irregular waves lapped against the side of the boat. Perhaps, the idea floated in his mind, perhaps they had reached the end of this journey. He turned that possibility over, and loosed a small, satisfied sigh. The boat had stopped. He was somewhere else. He could sleep now. From beneath his stupor, he recognized, with a vague apprehension, that if he were to become fully conscious at this moment, he would find himself in great pain. Why this should be so, he could not remember. Someone had tucked him in. He was not alone. When he woke, time enough then to remember, to ask questions, to sing again with that faint whisper of music that sounded in his mind as though from a far distance.

"'E be awake."

The Boatman grunted and swung Aedan's hammock away from the wall.

"Easy. Easy with the boy." The Boatman's voice was gruff. "'E's come through the fire and the river. 'E be a good'un. Careful!"

Willing his eyes to open, Aedan managed a slit-eyed look at the world before him as his body was hauled from the hammock. Two monstrous faces—blue and yellow and red and green—bent over him. His eyes widened in alarm, but even that involuntary action cost him. A jolt of pain loosed a cry of anguish from the depths of his searing mind.

"Quickly." A high voice keened above him, and the pain was once more banished behind some well-constructed barrier. Aedan tried to force his eyes open that merest slit once again, failed, and concentrated instead on keeping some sense of awareness pulled about him.

The shift in weight beneath him told him when those who carried him stepped from the ferryboat onto the dock—the hard boards ringing with the sound of crisp booted footfalls. Dry, then. His small triumph in gaining that much knowledge buoyed his spirits.

A great buzz of sound burst around them as his bearers carried him along the dock. Strange voices called out and others answered in a multitude of tongues—not one of which he understood. Now they traversed stone pavement; now his bearers spoke a smooth word here, there—and each time the sounds receded as, he guessed, the throngs which crowded the thoroughfare gave way for their procession.

The jingling of a bridle reached him, sweet smells, shrill laughter, a squabbling and scratching as a cock was shooed away. Sunlight dappling. Beneath his closed lids, he felt their passage into and out of the light, heard the brush of leaves against wall. Then the noises of the day were cut off. A cool breeze stirred along his cheekbones. The careful, quick strides of his carriers were muted, and then the boots rang out on stone, his head rolling to the right as they ascended a shallow flight of steps.

"Here." A single firm voice. Female. Middle years. Soft hands pulled at his wrappings, and he felt his body sinking into something weightless, soft. His muscles seemed eased of their stiffness as his body settled into that cloud. Concentrating, he attempted yet again to open his heavy lids and focus his gaze. Those glittering faces swam before him, the colors dazzling, blurring, and tiring him.

"Open."

Without thought, his lips parted and a trickle of wine wet his throat. Greedily, he licked at the droplets that beaded on his dry lips. The wine, like the bed in which he lay, brought comfort to his aches. Inside, his mind subsided into the same state of easement as his body.

"Enough."

The barest sigh escaped him as the cup was removed. Dimly he was aware of the muffled booted feet retreating, of someone seated beside him, before blessed sleep claimed him.

Aedan stirred in his chair as it was positioned with care in the sun. Three days' time since he'd awakened and already strength flowed back into body and mind. In another day he'd be able to stand. Then, Ashara said, he would have an audience with the Dogon himself. The Dogon. Who or what he was, Aedan could not guess. Where had the river run? Where had he ended? Below him a city stretched so far that he could not see the edges of it. Behind him lay a harbor encircled by a peninsula along which the city also sprawled. The harbor was vast. The mouth of the river—and, surely, he thought, it must be the fabled Dura—could scarcely be seen.

Picking up the gilded black cup from the table positioned beside his chair, Aedan sipped at his tea as he took in the vista spread before him. The city undulated up and down the dozen or more low hills that rose from the harbor's edge. Buildings rose likewise story upon story with graceful, swallow-like eaves dipping to earth. Everywhere, pockets of greenery flourished in parks and along wide avenues that thronged with a multitude of city-dwellers. An open-air theatrical troupe seen far below him in miniature was giving a performance to a packed crowd in a park. Elsewhere strange, brightly colored globes floated in the air like exotic faceless birds. Strung along the very rooftops of the huge structure beneath him, lanterns came on one by one to bolster the fading sun as small knots of people gathered in exquisite gardens.

And everywhere, the dark-clad ordinary folk went about their business—stopping in a hundred or more markets, bustling in and out of street after street of shops, pausing before corner vendors' stalls where the hungry could purchase instant gratification. Once in a while, the breeze would draw out the sounds of chiming bells or the strains of street musicians. There on the opposite hillside went a sinuous procession of monks—clad in one-shouldered robes of a brilliant marine-blue. Before them marched cadres of shuffling musicians with cymbals and bells and incense and banners. The jostling crowd on the street gave way before the endless parade. The light had paled further toward evening when his attendant wheeled him inside. Still, he saw, that slow procession below had not reached an end.

Nervous now, Aedan buttoned the stiff, gold brocaded fabric of his loose jacket over finely woven dark blue trousers. Supple slippers muffled his footsteps as he stood back from the pier mirror and raked his astonished eyes over a stranger's visage. The dark unruly curls had been neatly trimmed, the stubble of beard shaved, and the pallor of his skin eased by the caress of the sun and the food and drink he'd been coaxed to take.

Through the test of fire and of water. The half-remembered words of the Boatman came back to him, and he recognized, then, the straight back and weary eyes of the man he'd become. The hard, muscled body shifted and the brocade caught the light. His hands, steadied now, sketched a brief salute to the faint grin of the amused figure in the mirror. He would meet this Dogon with his head held high.

Ashara, in gleaming marbled robes of turquoise and white silk, fell into step before him as he left his chambers, his attendants falling in behind him. Ashara led them down an endless maze of corridors and stairwells until at last they stood before immense brass doors with the curious entwined circular emblem centered between the two doors—a symbol he had glimpsed again and again in their passage. Now, without a word or gesture from Ashara that he could see, those massive doors swung open with the barest whisper of sound. They advanced onto a landing that overlooked an enormous chamber. Before them, another stairway descended, covered with that same brilliant blue the monks had worn. The carpet rolled without end before them down the interminable length of the hall. Everywhere stood groups of people—gaudy and shining in splendid robes. Smoke, incense, and perfumes wafted up to where they stood. No one appeared to take the slightest notice of them.

Ashara stepped down, Aedan and his attendants following. Reaching the bottom of the stairs, a few curious faces turned to him, and he hoped his own startled thoughts were not revealed. What he had dismissed as the stuff of nightmare—those yellow and blue and red and green faces—was reality! Tattooed and painted faces stopped in mid-word, falling silent as he passed. Down, down the length of the great hall they passed at a sedate, measured walk, the throng falling quiet and regrouping as they passed.

At length Ashara approached the end of the hall. Here, a great, gilded dragon reared its magnificently carved head thirty feet into the air, wings outstretched as though protecting a disk-shaped seat clutched in the wicked, curved talons of the dragon's feet. Huge faceted sapphires set into the dragon's eyes fractured the light into a million glittering motes that danced in a fierce gaze which appeared to follow his every step. Aedan dropped his eyes to the occupant at repose upon the blue velvet cushions tumbled within the golden disk the dragon guarded.

A man of late-middle years, spare of bone and sinew with gaunt, sunken cheeks and eyes that burned into

Aedan's sat within the dragon's embrace. His pallor was all the more shocking against the unpainted face, the simple, resplendent white tunic and trousers of raw silk that he wore. An attendant knelt before him, proffering a tray from which the man removed a stemmed jade goblet. His voice rang out, strong and commanding, through the hushed hall as he addressed Aedan.

"Come forward, little dragon-brother!
Kneel before the fabled dragon-throne
Of the East. Drink of the dragon's blood
And take on his power! This is the fifth
Observation of the Quoran Dru."

Ashara stepped aside into the crowd. Aedan felt the hush of the hall weighing upon his shoulders. He advanced before that fierce, piercing gaze, bent one knee in a deep obeisance, rose and accepted the goblet from the Dogon. The shimmering burgundy liquid caught the light with a silken, seductive sheen. Wine. Without hesitation, Aedan drained the cup. Light and sound exploded about him as the throng gathered in the hall erupted into tumult.

Chapter 9

The slight clank of the slot in the door alerted Barak. Rousing himself from a half-sleep, he stumbled on hands and knees in the dark to the door, felt the precious tray, willing his eager hands to restraint. Once before in his haste, he'd spilled most of his water. He would not make the same mistake twice. Sinking down with his back to the door, he grasped the rough mug with shaking hands and took one measured mouthful of the tepid liquid. Setting the mug on the floor beside him, he felt the floor in front of the cell door and identified a bowl, a spoon, and a chunk of hard substance that he recognized from previous meals as a thin slice of stale bread. He willed himself to take slow bites, savoring the texture of the lump of porridge that filled a third of his bowl. The bread, if soaked in water, would become edible, if not palatable.

How many meals did this one make? More than ten now? He had been unconscious when brought into the Sindren temple compound, awakening he knew not how long after in this tiny, darkened cell. The darkness was absolute. Not only light, but sound itself was absent. He was naked and alone. At irregular intervals, meals were shoved through the slot in the bottom of the door, but even then no light entered the cell. He was, he reflected with growing terror, cut off from the world in every way that mattered. Blind, alone.... He bit off those tormenting thoughts even as he gnawed at his hunk of bread.

They had failed, there, if they'd thought to drive him mad! By the Light! He could still touch—his food, the floor, the walls around him, the slot in the door, the seams of the door, himself. He could talk and hear his words, though he was careful only to speak thoughts aloud that had no bearing on his quest or on his friends. Such small powers remained to him, gave solid reassurance that the outside world still existed, that he, Barak, still existed, that his companions would be carrying on the search for Aedan without him.

Yet, the more he thought about his predicament, the more puzzled he became at the motives behind the Corps' treatment of himself. And he wondered if they had other captives from that night. At least one other, he thought. But, why this slow torture? Did his captors, those shaven-headed priests of Da'a, hope that his accomplices would attempt a rescue? Ha! Obal, if he hadn't been taken also, would consider it, he knew, but Isman-Bati would know full well the futility of such an effort. No, his friends would be on their way, even now, searching for Aedan.

He drank off more of his water and sighed. That vision of the boat came to him again—when they had come so close to seeing their young charge. The twining pattern lashing the shelter to the barge. That detail had worried at him all his waking hours since he'd regained consciousness. He'd seen it before, he'd swear by the Light! Yet, when? And where? Had Obal been with him? Would Obal remember? Had any of those who'd won free that night also noticed it? His head sagging back against the door, Barak nursed the last mouthful of his water, then grimaced in pain. Had his captors put something into that miserable porridge to tear at his insides so? He dragged himself into the farthest corner of his cell, where the stench grew the longer he was confined here. How many days? He cursed the Sindren Corps and the god they served loud and long.

The Emperor's dog squatted on his haunches in the marketplace, sniffing like his namesake before biting into the thick, crusty pasty he'd just purchased. A small, diamond-faced monkey leapt from an overhead lattice that roofed a nearby stall into the top-heavy baskets of zandala melons carried by two dusky Mindar river traders. The baskets overbalanced, the golden globes rolling into the square, startling a young mare that reared in fright and sent half her cargo of rugs spilling awry from the cart she drew.

Assir grabbed for the mare's harness, crooning and soothing her with a few soft words as the Mindar traders leaped to salvage their melons and shook their fists at the chattering monkey, who took alarm at the sudden confusion and swung arm over arm through a lacemaker's kiosk. The artisan added her shrill tones to the melee as her delicate panels were sent flying in all directions. Several small boys gave chase to the monkey, sending the Emperor's dog sprawling in their exuberant pursuit.

Behind the horse-drawn cart, Obal and Shavi gathered the straying rolls of carpet. With one deft swipe the big man cuffed the Emperor's dog on the head as the young man strove to regain his balance. Thrusting the unconscious body into the cart, Obal and Shavi made quick work of covering the body with rolls of rugs. Shavi swung aboard the cart with a lightning grin, anchoring the goods, while Obal nodded to Assir. The little boys gave up their chase of the monkey as it scampered onto a roof before jumping down into a wide alley and disappearing from sight. The melon-sellers now removed and the monkey long gone, horse, cart, cargo, and attendants crossed the square at a slow, measured pace to disappear down that same wide alley.

The taking of the dog had gone just as planned, Obal reflected as he followed the cart. The Emperor's dogs were a select cadre of messengers drawn from each major province—the former the Five Crowns of Aranth—and from Mamut itself. Given his crest, this particular dog was a Halfern rider. Now what business, Isman had wondered to Obal on their way across the market plaza earlier, would such a one have in Altari-Maro? Bearing a message, perhaps, to the Sindren temple head? And was it paranoia to suppose that such a message must have a connection with the capture ten days ago of Barak and three others from the gathering? Was it possible that those whom Za-avan had sent to follow the Q'tar through the Naransai mountains had been alerted to the presence in the city of one of Aedan's companions? To this end, the dog had been taken. He would, Obal assured the cloth merchant with a grim determination, succeed in obtaining answers to these and other questions they might wish to put to the dog.

"Does your crest proclaim the truth?" Obal's voice, soft but menacing, greeted the wary, darting eyes of the Emperor's dog. "Are you then a man of Halfern?"

The man remained mute. He was young by the looks of him, rough about the edges as though a year ago he might have been any village child, flaunting his riding prowess at the autumn fair. Eyes narrowing, Obal stepped closer. His huge hand shot out. The young man flinched, but the giant before him turned his face with a gentleness which surprised him into the small circle of lantern light.

"By the stars of Zilla! Crispin Drue's middle son! What do you here, child" Obal's incredulous tones boomed out, and the dog's face widened in astonished response, his mouth falling open. Then he snapped it shut, his lower lip trembling although he fought with a visible effort to control it.

Obal drew up a chair, sat the young man down, then seated himself on an upturned barrel in the light of the lantern so that he could be seen. The others faded without a sound into the shadows.

"I'm sorry, son," Obal's voice was gruff when he spoke, "to have taken you so roughly. But needs must, when the cause is urgent." His shrewd eyes met those of the still silent young man. "Aye, Caskar, I know ye well. Who did they take, child, to hold thy tongue so well?"

Caskar's dark eyes blinked.

"Was't your ailing father Crispin?" Obal's eyes narrowed in thought. "Or, p'raps your sister Elspatta, a pretty little thing, comely as a rose, if I recall her rightly?"

The fine tumble of curls jounced as Caskar's head shot up.

"Elspatta and Rosetta!" he cried. "Both sisters! Into the temple." His words rushed out in an agony of tormented disbelief. "If I fail to return, if they think I have betrayed them! Obal, they will kill my sisters! Even now...." The boy turned a wretched face to the big man, panic rising in his eyes.

Isman and Nepentha conferred in hushed voices. Then Isman stepped into the light and touched Obal on the shoulder.

His doublet dusted off and a slight bruise swelling beneath his chin, the Emperor's dog presented himself before the temple gate and was admitted after a sharp glance at his crest. Once inside, Caskar went directly to his barracks and splashed water on his face before making his way to the mess hall. Dunkil, a dog from Tabor, the northern neighbor of Halfern, grunted an acknowledgment without lifting the tankard of mead from her lips.

The Sindren Corps housed the messengers away from temple acolytes in separate quarters near the stables. The dogs ate together, bunked together, sometimes fought amongst one another, until a return message was sent back to the Emperor's stooges in the provinces. Few came of their own accord to the service for the founding was meager and death not an unknown outcome between the machinations of the Emperor's feuding ranks and those of the Sindren Corps. Dunkil, a few years older than Caskar, rode for the life of her elder brother Dafyd—a healer known far and wide on the northern slopes of the Naransai in Tabor province. Now Dafyd's days were confined to his village and Dunkil rode under the Emperor's colors.

Dunkil drained her mead and nudged Caskar's elbow.

"Did not the very ground rise up to meet you, youngster?" The twinkle in her eye belied her rangy, solemn features.

"Aye," Caskar replied blandly. "A twisted street it was, with a monkey leaping into the fruit baskets, upsetting the whole market. Lucky I was to get away with my hide intact." He grinned.

"How goes your mount today, Dunkil?" he asked, meeting his companion's gaze with wide eyes and ignoring her startled glance. "I'd be most happy to pick out his hoof, if you think it would help."

Pushing her now empty tankard away, Dunkil clapped Caskar on the shoulder.

"Aye, another pair of eyes and a hand on that hoof would set my mind at rest. Shall we attend to him now, then?"

Caskar picked up a hoof of the tall, rawboned stallion that Dunkil rode and examined it with a critical eye. He might have an ulterior motive for speaking with her in private, but one's mount meant the difference between successfully delivering a message and the life of one's hostages. Dunkil steadied her kerser stallion's head, and spoke in a low voice that carried no further than Caskar's ears.

"Out with it youngster. No one is near. What really happened to your face today?"

Without straightening, Caskar related his mishap in the market. Dunkil whistled under her breath, her brown eyes wide.

"What made them set you free?"

Caskar put the stallion's hoof down and stood up, his eyes holding those of his friend.

"They asked one thing only, Dunkil. Information. Are the prisoners who were brought in ten days ago still living? If so, where are they held?"

The Tabor woman pursed her lips, then spoke a quieting word to her restless horse. Caskar picked up another hoof and dislodged a bit of gravel as another of the Emperor's dogs walked by. A sharp-faced, bearded Mamut man, he retrieved a saddle. They watched in taut silence as he led his great bay horse from its stall and out into the courtyard.

"Surely," Dunkil's low voice barely reached her companion's ears, "your countryman cannot hope to free the prisoners?"

Caskar put down the hoof he held and shrugged. Dunkil scratched her throat in a nervous gesture.

"I've been here two weeks, Caskar. All prisoners are kept in the north wing. No one goes in save for two priests from the kitchens—never the same two and never at the same hour. Four prisoners came in at dawn ten days ago—two unconscious. So far," her voice caught in her throat and her whisper was hoarse, "there have been no fresh fires in the crematory."

"I thank you, Dunkil." He grunted, running a hand along the stallion's neck. The spotted kerser gave a soft whicker and nuzzled his hand. Caskar flexed his tired shoulders, shoved the damp fair curls from his eyes, met those of his fellow rider.

"Perhaps I can return the favor, elder sister," his voice trailed off and he eyed the russet-haired Tabor rider in a thoughtful silence for a moment. "They asked one thing, Dunkil, but for this small favor, they gave much in return." His slender face lit up with an inner fire. Dunkil's eyes narrowed in speculation, the heavy braids swinging about her face as she bent nearer.

"Gold?" she demanded. Not from greed, Caskar understood at once, but gold! With enough, one could sometimes buy a hostage's freedom with a few discreet bribes.

Caskar shook his head, grinning.

"Better!"

"Better than gold?" Dunkil stepped closer. "What treasure is this youngster?"

Caskar's grin disappeared, his face solemn, his young voice deepening.

"Would you like to carry a second message on your return to Tabor? An unauthorized one—one of hope, one to be spread at each stop you make along the way."

At Dunkil's puzzled look, Caskar gave a furtive glance around the stables. No one was near. He mouthed the words clearly.

"The Q'tar." The older dog seized his arm with a convulsive gesture.

"What are you saying, child?"

"Yes!" The boy's voice quivered with excitement, breaking. "He walks among us even now, Dunkil. The Corps," with another glance about the stable, Caskar lowered his voice even further, "suspect this and they seek him. These are *his* friends secured in the cells of the Sindren hold here."

Dunkil's gaunt face was transformed. With tight control, she reined in that surge of overpowering relief with an effort. The Light had not forsaken them, not withdrawn from life. Hope existed!

"The Q'tar!" she breathed the name with reverence. "But," quick brown eyes raked Caskar's shining face, "what if his friends should talk, reveal his whereabouts?" Her hand went to the dagger in her belt. Caskar checked that innate response.

"Nay, be not hasty, Dunkil!" He cautioned his friend. "They cannot reveal what they do not know. But listen, like a spring-melt creek running to the river, we must spread the word as we go. Do you know any others among us who can be trusted to do the same? Any Dravan,

Almeridian, or Elfarn riders?" He thought quickly. "I dare not hope that any of those of Mamut would be receptive."

Dunkil tugged at a stray braid. "Nantis of Elfarn—word has it his sister disappeared in the high reaches of the Naransai, seeking the holy refuge of the Light. But of Dravan, I know of no one."

She took a coarse blanket from the stall railing and settled it with care over her stallion.

"Perhaps," Caskar added with a sly glint in his eye, "Nantis will know something of them."

"Yes." A brief smile came and went as Dunkil met that look.

"Come along, youngster. Needs must we meet curfew without question. But I think your trickling creek may yet reach flood stage!"

Barak lay huddled in the darkness, feeling his ragged breath going in and out. Taking a deep breath, he tried to steady his breathing. Yet, the foul stench of his own waste was near overpowering. Then came the sound he waited for—the faint creak of the slot in the door as it opened. He had tried, two meals ago, eating only the bread and porridge. It had made no difference to his raging digestive system. That last meal, then, he'd finished the water and left the rest untouched. Now his stomach gnawed at his backbone, and he had only sharpened the dull ache of hunger into an overt pain—all to no avail. The awful cramping had not relented.

This time he made no move to reach for the tray. If they had not sacrificed him to Da'a outright, if they had not come into his cell to torture him, then their purpose, to succeed, must need him alive a while longer. The only control he held over his situation lay in this: what if their prisoner refused to eat? How, he wondered, would his captors react? Surely someone would come to check on him. He might be able to provoke a response. If they killed him, then he would be free from this pain and uncertainty. And he would no longer be a tool in their hands.

Beyond that, he could not plan. Pushing his thoughts away, he sat up with an effort and felt for the tray. He willed his resistant hands to tilt the precious water from the mug. Once done, he pushed the crust of bread away and set the bowl of porridge by the door slot. The lack of sound so far during his imprisonment had made him think he was alone. But what if that's what they wanted him to think?

Pulling himself close to the door, Barak closed his tired eyes and wiped his sweating palms on his shirt before he began to beat the heavy crockery mug against the wooden tray. Clunk! Clunk! Clunk! How long he kept up his efforts, he did not know. The last dull thud seemed to echo. At the sound, he roused himself. His own hands were stilled. Yes! The dull thud came again. Someone else lived! Someone answered! With rising excitement, he clanged the mug against the tray once more and listened for the response to come.

So. More than one of them. Fed at the same time, too. With a grim satisfaction, Barak slumped against the wall. The knowledge might not set them free, but there was a certain measure of comfort to be taken from that first, albeit tenuous contact with another living soul. He closed his eyes against the darkness. Darkness. The absence of light. His eyes jerked open as the realization dawned. In the hollow, he remembered, they had used candles to channel the light in the heart of the night. He struck his fist against his thigh in frustration. Not having felt the call to a spiritual life, his past had steered him clear of any knowledge of the calling of the light. Was the power of light then defeated by this darkness in which he was held captive? If only he knew more!

Mari-Isman kept one eye on the antics of her youngest—Sherat and Kapura—as she chose a healthy bunch of dark green satil leaves for the supper. Crisped in cold water, the leaves would make a base for sliced cooked tubers and rice—a simple repast. The weaver appeared not to notice the young man reaching across the red-fleshed pears, calling out a sharp reminder to Sherat to keep an eye on his sister around the charcoal seller's brazier. Turning back to the stall, she murmured a polite 'excuse me' as she decided that pears would be a welcome end to supper and found herself entangled for a moment with her fellow shopper. Corralling her youngsters, she shepherded them on their way.

Caskar bit into his sun-warmed pear. The sweet red juice flowed welcome on his tongue. Lifting his face to the sun, he grinned with pleasure. Word had come. Tomorrow Dunkil rode for Tabor. And no word for himself. That must mean, he thought with contentment as he set off in the direction of the warm smell of new loaves of bread, that the Sindren's prisoners had not yet set them on the trail of the Q'tar. The Corps must not know for certain, must only suspect that he moved through the world. Why else let the captives live this long? Those captives should have been tortured and dispatched to the crematory long before this time. Did the Sindren priests hope to draw in their prisoners co-conspirators? Perhaps the Q'tar himself? For Obal had said, 'he' comes.

Shavi tugged absently at his beard; Nepentha sat with hands clasped about her knee, her gaze unfocused. Jani, the jeweler's apprentice, worked before her bench, humming an aimless tune under her breath. Obal stood at once, tense in every muscle as Mari-Isman and the cloth merchant were admitted by Quan Matar, the cadaverous granary clerk.

"They live." Isman answered Obal's unspoken question.

"Then it is so," Nepentha observed with brows drawn together . "Those carrion-eaters who serve Da'a hold the people of the light in hopes of entrapping the rest of us." Her great dark eyes blazed with contempt and she jumped up from her seat. "In hopes of fetching the Q'tar into their hands!"

Quan Matar folded his lanky body into a sitting position next to Jani on her workbench, watching Nepentha from deep, shadowed eyes. Jani, bird-like, turned about on her stool at Nepentha's words. Shavi raised his hands, as if to calm the tailor's daughter, then shrugged and addressed the group at large.

"We here are clearly torn in two directions. First and foremost, to find the Q'tar and aid him in any way that we can. Second," he lifted an admonitory hand as Nepentha made an involuntary movement of protest. "Second," he repeated with steel in his voice as Obal bit off whatever he meant to say, "how to rescue our comrades from a Sindren cell."

"And it seems to me," Jani offered, shaking her head, "that we are lost in both directions. If only the seeking had not been broken!"

An ominous rumble escaped Obal at this thought.

"The past cannot be reshaped," Isman rebuked the younger woman with his accustomed gentleness. "Two tasks lie before us. Then needs must we break our forces into two parts."

"Aye," Quan Matar agreed. "Neither task will be accomplished by sheer force of numbers. Say I, then, that we divide our numbers—one group to seek and one to stay."

"And if," Nepentha spat the words out in her anger, "we fail to save those here, then half our force will have wasted time and perhaps their lives when we might have saved the Q'tar instead! I say we cut our losses here and go now!"

Mari-Isman put out a hand to clasp Obal's clenched fist. She addressed the tailor's daughter with a calmness that held Obal's retort in check.

"You know best for yourself, Nepentha, that the Light calls each of us to our own path. You will go. I remain."

"And I," Shavi added. "How could the harbormaster disappear without arousing comment?"

"Aye." Quan Matar stood. "I go." An unexpected grin lightened his lugubrious features. "A clerk will not be missed."

Jani giggled.

"Nor will a jeweler's apprentice." She looked with regret at the unfinished necklace before her on the bench, then at the group before her. "I go."

"I stay also," Isman informed them. "Late winter is not known to be a buying time for new woolens."

Obal, torn between their two objectives, formed one last appeal.

"But how can we search for Aedan," he asked, his voice pleading, "when we don't know where to search?"

Nepentha regarded him with surprise.

"We are the seekers, Obal. We do not ride the light like some, but we are the seekers. Once away from this sink of Sindren stench, we will seek the Q'tar by reaching out to those who hold the light."

"Then," the big Halfern man spoke from the heart with relief, ignoring her superior tone, "you will have no need of me, for I am no seeker. I stay."

"Good." If Nepentha did not speak her thought aloud, it was clear upon her countenance. Her glance flicked over her companions. "Much time has been lost. Let us prepare and be on our way before nightfall." Like a raptor converging on a brood of gangli chicks, she flapped her arms at Quan Matar and Jani.

"The blind leading the blind," Obal muttered to himself, caught Isman's raised brow, and mustered a sheepish grin.

Chapter 10

The high winds of the Dravanian altiplano bleached the warmth from the very marrow of her bones. Jennet hunched deeper into her heavy, felted chalpatera, oblivious by now to its goat-like smell, and waited for the signal. Over the continuous whining of wind through whip-sharp grasses, she caught the silver-thinned notes of a flute, piercing and hollow, then the faint echo was lost under the crunch of her boots on the rocky soil.

By the shore of the inky mountain lake, a cluster of huts huddled against the cold. Most of the Dravanians lived in the three great valleys which ran down from the mountain foothills to the Western ocean. Only in those three valleys was there water enough to irrigate fields and provide for the needs of cities and towns. Beyond the green-ribboned valleys lay a desert so barren that it had been all but abandoned time out of mind by the valley-dwellers. Two of the Dravanian tri-capitals rested in the resource-rich mouths of the north and south rivers, while the third capital clung to the foothills and their lucrative mines of precious metals. Poqwatl, Laltepoch, and Intalpa secured the realm like three exotic lilies in a field of daisies.

Yet, in the high mountains and the desert, the Quettar tribes roamed, ignored with disdain by the complacent valley-farmers and bureaucrats. Coming only into the fringes of the valleys, the Quettar traded crafts and tubers for grain and fruits and cotton, and sometimes younger sons to the matrons of the valley towns, where a woman could take more than one husband. True, brothers more often shared a wife, but where there were no brothers, one could be adopted. And the desert men were dark and comely and hard workers.

Just such men—young and old—stared now at Jennet as she put back her hood at Patar's side. Not for the Quettar the polyandrous unions of the valleys. They had no farmlands or businesses to hold in trust for one set of heirs. Instead, these men stood shoulder to shoulder with their womenfolk and eyed her with bold glances. Here in the village of Quettin, the local tribes were sedentary fisherfolk and weavers of reeds, unlike most of their nomadic, pastoral cousins. Jennet returned their stares with interest as space was cleared at a rough-hewn table and they were invited to share the villager's hospitality.

Proud, dark women sat among their men as equals. Jennet learned in the following days that a woman could take a spouse as readily as a man, provided the spouse-to-be was agreeable and the *pridari* was paid. In her old world of village, as among most of the peoples of the Five Crowns of Aranth, the *pridari* was given to the bride's parents to compensate them for the loss of a valued worker. Among the Quettar, children belonged to the household, claiming kin to both sets of relatives and as likely to join whichever kin-group best suited to their needs and talents as they became adults.

Now they broke bread with the strangers and passed steaming bowls of soup rich with the clear-fleshed lake fish and lowland vegetables. When all who sat at the table had been sated, the tall old man called Dakash—his warm, sable brown eyes unfaded by age although his braid lay thick and silver down his back—rose and poured a drop of ruby liquid from the carafe he was offered into a cup. This he set before their guests. The same minuscule portion he poured into his own cup before raising it high. Silence fell over the crowd. While the language of the northern countries was foreign to this Quettar's tongue, his words flowed out in deep, resonant tones. Jennet was not surprised to find Patar translating Dakash's speech for her.

"We who are the Quettar praise the Light. May it never dim in the mountain fastness that is home!" Dakash drank, Patar and Jennet following suit. "Listen well, people of Quettin. Even now the valley-dwellers of Intalpa seek to control our Quettar cousins who dwell near—seeking to tax their labor and the fruits of their labor." Dark eyes flashed with anger in the crowd and voices grumbled. The old man lifted a hand for quiet.

"We who are far removed from the valleys, still we watch and we know these things. We know the red banners and the growing enclaves of black-robed monks who swell the coastal capitals and gain a foothold in Intalpa.

"Yet, we are still the Quettar, the free people." A general murmur of approval flowed about them. "We have," here oblique glances and sly smiles met Dakash's words, "yielded to their demands only on the surface. Now," the white brows rose and the voice commanded all attention, "comes word that hope lives! Now must we unite with those other peoples of the north countries and push back this black pestilence of the Sindren Corps! No longer may we hold aloof in our mountain places!

"The Q'tar is known!"

A profound silence greeted his proclamation. 'We are doomed,' Jennet thought with despair, her small face pinched with weariness and defeat. 'All for naught!' Near the fire, the flute-player Utari loosed a trill of soft notes so like a chuckle that Jennet started. First one, then another of the silent Quettar raised hands joined to those of their neighbor and the shout they gave forth near lifted the thatch from the roof.

"Q'tar! Q'tar! Q'tar!"

A second flute chimed in with the first, then another, then a soft drum. The villagers lifted their hands and their voices in a song whose words may have been foreign to Jennet, but whose import was crystalline—glad tidings and joy resounded. The swaying bodies moved without signal into a dance, rank upon rank, until Patar and Jennet were swept from their seats into the measure.

Under the clear light of a Hunter's moon, Jennet pulled the hood of her chaltapera across the pale oval of her face like a veil and motioned for Utari to recede her. Utari, the gamin-faced flute player, had joined them in their perilous trek through the mountains, spreading word of the Q'tar from village to village. Tonight, however, they were involved in a little direct action as they moved down from the altiplano into the upper reaches of the Laltepoch valley. Here the Sindren Corps had moved upstream like some tenacious, unwholesome school of fish intent on spawning. The capital, Laltepoch, sat on the coast like an overfed arthropod, drawing the lifeblood from the villages and towns that laced the wide valley. Here in the southernmost valley the village-farmers grew a small-grained cousin of wheat—spaeta—sweet and tasty and much-prized to the north and east. Now the good farmers tithed not only to their capitol, but also to the Corps.

The taxed grain was stored in granaries spaced at regular intervals across the landscape. One of these, overfull to bursting, cast a rounded shadow into the night. Utari's flute trilled like the echo of a satah bird, then Patar ghosted by Jennet as swiftly as the satah's flight. Jennet remained in position until Utari's fluted call came a second time. The adobe-bricked walls of the squat-towered granary still carried the heat of the day's warmth as Jennet pressed against the brick. Opposite her, Patar should be in place. Utari would sound a warning if anyone approached. Who would? The full granary was a sign of the Corps' complacency. The valley-folk paid without a murmur. That thought caught at Jennet for a moment. What if the Sindren priests retaliated here in the nearby small village hamlets? She felt Patar's thought guiding her senses, then 'saw' as if she stood before him, the Sindren guard sitting at the gate relaxed yet fully alert. No one had approached, much less passed through the gate before the granary. So he would report when questioned.

Reassured, she pressed her palms to her heart and wished for the light to come to her. She cupped it and shaped it into a tiny, flickering flame, setting the image atop the honey-brown spaeta heaped with the tower. With Patar's will and Utari's flute, the spark held and grew, the small grains crisping before the heat. Long before the Sindren guard gathered his black robe from the dust to stand aghast before the fiery granary, Jennet, Patar, and Utari had fled in opposite directions to make their separate ways to a rendezvous at the village of Quetapl on the edge of the altiplano.

Day came as a narrow amorphous band of lighter gray against the eastern horizon. Jennet lay in that shifting state between full sleep and awakening, when dreams spin a free-fall of images winding through emotion and memory and imagination. Flames red as the anger of the Sindren Corps leapt to meet the sky—the sweet spaeta burned hot and quick, fueling a nightmarish vision in which every flame became a face that worried at her heels as she fled west to the safety of the altiplano. The faces of her foster brother Yostli and Elder Makur from her village loomed against darkness, then Baxti the cat from the City of Light—his eyes growing huge and his mouth opening wide to bare sharp fangs. Restless and tossing in her sleep, Jennet made a small, protesting sound. Why had all that was familiar and dear turned on her?

The scarlet flames popped and crackled in her dreams. A large, robust man reached powerful, compact fingers towards her neck, before another flame sparked and a strange man's visage rose before her. This face wore a faint smile that beckoned her to safety. A hooked nose was prominent in that thin, dark ascetic face. One earlobe was hung with a tiny red star that pulsed and flickered as the man's head turned, his smile fading to a look of urgent concern.

Hurry-hurry-hurry as the fire crawled behind her, now red, now black. Yet with the crazy logic of a dream, the faster she tried to go, the slower her gait became. At last she approached the dark-featured man and the haven he offered. To her horror, his features began to change even as she stood frozen before him—the mouth falling inward and the eyes sunken, a blackness consuming the smooth contours of that face from within. A Sindren shell covered by a mask of care? Who could she trust? Where could she turn? The fire of her dream edged closer, surrounding her.

When it seemed as if the nightmare must wake her, Jennet relaxed. Flames encircled her as she stood immobilized, yet did not engulf her. Instead, their flickering warmth played across her body like leaf-dappled shadows, caressing and tender. Light! And love. The flames could only hurt her when she failed to look beyond their destructive power, knowing, remembering how that same clean burning, that same sharp edge of light could salve the soul. Light!

A gentler sigh roused her from the depths of her dreams, and she looked out from half-opened eyes to see the that the dawn had grown to early morning even as she fought to wake from her nightmare. And what other image had caught at her sleep-entangled thoughts? Some hint and drift of love still lingered. She closed her eyes at the sudden jolt of pain that thought brought her. The specific, gentle love she would not personify. *He* would not be there when she opened her eyes. No point in indulging herself in that particular idle, frustrating dream. Time to bestir herself.

Utari's brown and green chalpatera floated in the mist before her. The searing cold ate at her now until even in sleep, curled before a fire between Patar and Utari, her skin cooled and she woke daily to shivering. All the food she could consume served only to chase away the cold, hold it back. Not a spare ounce of flesh clung to her now, and she looked as hard and tough and brown as the rocks she climbed among—throwing a resentful glance at her companions now and then. Utari—born and bred to the high mountains—kept breath enough on the roughest slopes to trill his flute and set her stubborn soul to motion, one weary foot in front of the other. For all his age, Patar matched the boy pace for pace. Only the deepening furrows of his forehead betrayed the strain wearing on him from their incessant march deeper and deeper into the Beyar Mountains that separated Dravan from Tabor.

Here they dared not travel on the light. Best to not advertise themselves until they could be sure of a welcome, so they went on foot from one remote village to another. The higher they climbed, the fewer the villages clinging to gorges a mile or more above the narrow, winding valleys. They passed on their message and each village was left to decide for themselves how or whether to act on the knowledge that the Q'tar was moving out in the world. The Sindren enclave in the lower valley, through the help of paid informers and swift retaliation, had pinpointed the general area from whence discontent had spread. To defy the Sindren Corps could mean extermination of entire villages.

Like a desert hound, nose to the ground, slavering and hungry for the kill, the Corps had sent a select cadre to hunt down the source of the pestilence. The three fled before the hunters on foot, hoping not to draw the Sindren hounds' attention to any particular place. They clung to the faint hope that the villagers would be able to retreat if the Corpsmen ventured this far into the mountains and could avoid lieber-sabers drawn on the innocent. And that, Jennet grunted as a stone gave beneath her foot and she came down with bruising force on one knee, was why she kept going, even if this was the price she must pay. Patar was right. The Corps would never suspect anyone foolish enough to try the descent into Tabor from the hostile Beyar slopes, near the very heart of the Mamut Empire. That was a grim satisfaction at the moment.

Utari's flute sang—the sound as sweet as water sparkling in stained glass patterns over smooth stream cobbles. Jennet massaged her cramped, cold toes, the pale blonde fall of hair loosed for once and fanning forward as she bit her lip and let the music guide her thoughts away from the hunger and fear that gnawed at her in equal measure. In that few seconds of concentration, her breath caught. Wide-eyed, stock-still, she stared into space for a measureless moment, then fought with all her might her need to throw wide the net of her thoughts, woven of light and loosed from time and space. Down, down, she fought that eagerness, that frantic reaching. Fought it to darkness and a precarious blankness of mind and thought.

"Jennet! Jennet-sweet!"

Firm hands tugged at her clenched fists pressed hard against her face. Patar pulled her fists free and shook her until her eyes showed recognition and a bleak, despairing pain that tore at his heart. With a cry, she buried her face against his shoulder as sobs shook her. Utari, his flute laid aside, spitted the game hens Patar had brought, his dark eyes intent only upon the job before him. Flute sang and gates opened. It was not for him to control or interfere.

"He's hurt, Patar." Jennet forced back the tears, pushed the hair back from her forehead. "He needs me, and I am here."

"You've done as need be, Jennet. To do otherwise would be to lead those others to him." Patar grimaced, took the hard, flat bread and mug of sweet tea offered by

Utari. Taking a deep drink, he shot a speculative look from Utari to Jennet. He knew that Jennet had been soul-tied to the boy Aedan by her village elders. It had been needful to have someone wholly of the light to guide the Q'tar to the City of Light. The Q'tar, after all, was neither of the light nor of the dark, but a living vessel who came pure of heart when there was need. Else he could not have come through the test of the falls before entering Abri-Hataro with Jennet.

With certainty he also knew that the soul-tie had been broken by the Lady in the Abri-Corazon. And the Q'tar had gone on his pathway towards the hour of need. When—or where—that hour might come, no one knew. But how, then, should this little flicker of light that was Jennet, how was it that she still touched the path of the Q'tar?

Jennet, aware of Patar's thoughtful gaze, made a show of bending over her boots, securing the laces before making quick work of braiding her hair. In a few minutes, all business once more, she held her bread for her share of the small tough hens snared by Patar.

"They are below us in the village."

Utari's swift, guarded glance sought Patar's face as Jennet looked away. She hunched one shoulder closer to the banked coals, drained her own mug of tea, and swallowed the bitter disappointment that ate at her without a protest. The surest path to *him* lay to the south—skirting the edges of the Great Dry Swamp to the sea beyond.

As if echoing her thoughts, Patar repeated. "They are below, in the village. We must strike farther north, my friends. Towards the Tabor Plains. If we are lucky, we can slip south again through the Mil-mille lakes and across the Settern river into Halfern."

"I should have liked," Utari grinned, "to have seen this place where a swamp can be dry."

Patar reached out and tousled the young man's hair.

"For league upon league it stretches. Once it must have been truly wet, but now, some change of climate over the generations has drawn off most of the moisture. Its sources of water choked off until it lies a muck-filled, slimy world from which foul odors escape and mournful cries are heard at nightfall."

Utari's dark eyes rounded and his hand patted at his flute with a nervous, protective gesture. Jennet reached for her pack. Time was slipping away while they ran before the Sindren hounds. How did the Corps keep one step behind them? Relentless. Almost as if those servants of the dark could follow the light! She stopped that unhealthy train of thought. Where she and her companions ran, hope flourished. Where hope lived, they had not failed. Shrugging on her pack, she kicked dirt over the meager warmth of their fire.

"Come, Utari." Patar flicked a thumb at the Quettar youth. "We have need of you and your flute."

A rustling of leaves scattered the thin, thready song of Utari's flute. Like a rope, twisted of the light and flung into the air, his flute wove a noose that brought in their prey.

Jennet crouched lower into the underbrush as another crackle of sound reached her ears. Then the noise stopped. With caution, she raised her head, met Patar's eyes from the other side of the swale. Utari swung down from his perch.

A Sindren Corpsman—newly recruited from the looks of his stubbled jaws and soft middle—slumped to his knees. Eyes unfocused, mouth slack, he seemed yet to hear that undertone of music which had sent a little quiver along Jennet's own stomach muscles.

Patar Q'an squatted before the recruit, motioned to Utari. Flute sang once more—a nameless, aimless, wandering tune that looped and repeated and danced away into the night. Their captive never moved.

"Son of Da'a," Patar's eloquent eyes flared with distaste as he spoke the traditional title, but his voice was steady and commanding, "what is your purpose in these hills?"

Silence. Then the man seemed to recollect his voice and made answer.

"We hunt the infidels who spread the seed of discontent among the children of Da'a." The hoarse whisper came as rote as a schoolchild's first numbers.

"You shall surely be glorified," Patar replied. "Tell me, how do you keep so closely to the infidels? Are they not fierce wizards and magicians?"

A small sigh escaped the Sindren corpsman.

"He sees."

The man lapsed again into silence.

They waited.

"Who sees?" Patar prompted.

"Da'a! The great and merciless one!" Once more, the pat answer came.

Patar grimaced in frustration. Jennet could feel sweat beading on her cheeks.

"Through whose eyes does Da'a see?"

The recruit's face puckered as though he might cry. His voice lowered even further.

"Gagues is his chosen. When the red heart of the stone is opened, Gagues sees. Like fire in the night...." The whisper died.

Patar reached out a hand and closed the man's eyes. The recruit slumped onto his side and began to snore.

"Come!" Patar beckoned to Utari, silencing the flute. "We will leave this one behind. His words have given us much to think upon once we are well away from here."

From her vantage point high among the concealing foliage of a stout, leafy oak, Jennet watched the slow, thorough progress of the Sindren ranks below her as they beat the tall grass at the stream's edge in a methodical pattern. Signaling to Patar, she climbed down and swung herself free from the lowest limb.

"Why is it," Jennet wondered aloud as she rejoined her companions, "that we cannot lose these hounds?"

Patar straightened his weary shoulders.

"Somehow, this 'red heart' seems to lead them directly to us, no matter how we seek to misdirect our trail."

The image of a dark-visaged, scowling face crossed Jennet's mind—a man who wore a scarlet star in his earlobe. She shivered, raised her chin, and related to Patar and Utari the tale of her nightmare.

"Patar," she hesitated and gulped, "I do not know who this man might be, but hear me. We must split up and see if those who hunt behind us do so also, or whether like an arrow loosed from a bow, they follow but one."

"And then?" Patar asked, his eyes flickering from Jennet to Utari and back again to the girl.

"Then we shall decide," Jennet's expression was bleak, "whether one of us is to be caught so the rest may go free."

"No!" Utari protested with dismay. "To this I cannot agree." His slender body quivered with indignation. "Have we not now the safety," his dark eyes implored of Patar, "to call the light to us and be gone from this threat?"

The older man passed a grimy hand across the unruly dark curls grown even grayer since their trek through Dravan.

"If we go forth from here," he rejoined at last, "we shall not know the face of our enemy."

"But," Utari's denial slashed at them in his frustration, "our enemy is the Sindren Corps. Is that not all the knowledge we need?"

"Nay," Jennet answered for her companion. "We must know more. Why are these hounds so bent upon us? Learning this, we may be able to eliminate the threat and so serve the Q'tar and the side of the light."

Patar nodded.

"And when we serve, we must not flee."

Utari shook his head as if he did not like that thought.

"Come!" Patar Q'an clapped their Quettar friend on the shoulder. "There are other ways to bait a trap than with a sacrificial lamb!" His even white teeth flashed in a fierce, mirthless grin. "In the next wide vale on the shores of Lake Aleri, we will find the crofts of a gentle fisherfolk. Go there, Jennet, and wait two days. Utari and I will draw off and watch, then join you."

"No!" Jennet hunched her shoulders against the deepening chill of the breeze. "I think you know as well as I which way those hounds of Da'a will turn their noses. I can't draw them to those good folk!"

"Do not underestimate the power of the Light," Patar rebuked her gently. "Did you not leave the City of Light blessed by the Lady herself? Think you that you have been forsaken in your moment of need?"

A slow flush suffused her wan features, then Jennet ducked her head, gripped her comrades' hands in a wordless message of care, and turned without a word to the shoreside trail.

Bird-like, flute whistled and Patar showed his face once to acknowledge the Quettar youth's signal. It had not taken two days to realize that Jennet was indeed the target of the Corps' troops fanned out behind them. The hunters had converged like a flung spear upon a single trail, not distracted in any measure by those two who watched from concealment. Camped in clear view, the

Sindren troop appeared to await the morning before approaching the village of Aleri fisherfolk.

Patar crept with as much stealth as he could manage into and out of shadows as clouds formed above the moisture laden breezes off Lake Aleri and at times obscured the pared shape of the waning moon. With silent cautiousness, he neared the low stone containment wall that set one house apart from its neighbors, the lane, and the shore path down to the lake. Not a village cur remarked upon his passage, not a cat stirred.

In the space of a second's hesitation, Patar felt himself gripped from two sides, his neck arched back. A quick gleam of silver marked the blade at his throat. Without thought, he gripped the hand holding that knife so close to life or death for him.

"Bring him!" A curt voice ordered. "And the small nightbird."

A grotesque shape moved past Patar's line of vision into the dimming moonlight, and he realized it was Utari, flung over someone's shoulder. The monstrous humpedback figure strode before him and his captors.

Inside the central village hall, torchlight smoked in a ring about the walls, filling the hall. Patar's eyes tightened as he resisted that momentary blindness. Sighted again, he met the troubled gaze of Jennet. She was seated amidst the central knot of figures filling the room. One glorious lady, chestnut tresses graying in dramatic locks, stood, commanding silence with a raised hand. Her stout body trembled for a moment beneath the enveloping, knitted clay-colored tunic and breeches she wore.

"Ho! Patar Q'an!" Her delighted howl of greeting rang in the rafters of the village hall. The woman strode forward to pump Patar's hand and encircle him in her arms with a vise-like embrace. Her fellows holding Patar faded back into the crowd.

"We have your fledglings," the Aleri woman waved a hand. "See, the little night-singer stirs." Utari sat up on the bench where he had been deposited, clutching his flute.

"I have brought you a night's amusement, Jotak." Patar grin reminded Jennet of a wolf. She shivered. "They wait for dawn and the light."

Jotak shook with delight.

"Shall the light disappoint them?"

"Ho!" A ferocious shout swept the crowd of Aleri.

"Patar," Jotak urged him forward, "your two chicks will be taken to Sieri's craft to await you after our revels. Will you show us where this school of flesh-eaters lurks?"

Jennet, accompanied by two slender, doe-eyed Aleris—alike enough to be twins, watched as long spears were snatched up, each gleaming as the light struck the embedded crystalline barbs that bit into the pale white wooden shafts.

"Buti-scales," one of the Aleri remarked, catching her glance. Each lance tip, passed through a torch, seemed to catch the fire within those clear tangs.

"Fiercest of the sea-wolves," the other Aleri added. "The Sea-Aleri trade them for taipi chains." A finger pointed to a nearby figure that shook a length of gray-green filaments from a hafted handle into a container of water. Aiming, he flicked it at a melon. Like a living attacker, the taipi filaments clung tightly, tautened. Jennet shivered as the melon split under the pressure.

"Leader... red stone...." She caught fragments of Patar's hushed conversation with Jotak as he bent over a scroll of fawn-colored flexible paper held before Jotak. With a decisive jab of a forefinger, he pinpointed the position of the Sindren Corps' night encampment. Her minders led the way out of the village hall and down the shore road to the lake.

Tucked in the prow of Sieri's craft like a basket of fish, Jennet fought back her fear for Patar, made Utari comfortable in the crook of her arm, and breathed a quiet sigh of relief as their two Aleri watchdogs were joined by three others. The craft was loosed from its moorings and Sieri poled them out into the lake beyond the last of the Aleri boats. Here they would wait for Patar's and the villagers' return, safely out of range of a lieber-saber's beam. Not, Jennet thought as she stole a glance at those deceptive Aleri profiles watching the shore, that the Corps stood much of a chance of using those fire-born weapons. Weariness settled over her and she tightened her arm about Utari, who remained quiet but alert. She permitted herself one small flicker of worry. Where was Aedan tonight? Somehow in her thoughts he was never the Q'tar—only Aedan. And that was more than enough.

Chapter 11

"Dopan." Aedan marveled at the sound of it. The capital of the Eastern Empire flowed like a quilt of many colors and threads along the creamy sands that bordered the Inland Sea. His journey had ended in the heart of legend. The heavy crimson silk of his shirt rustled as he turned away from the window. What he had first thought to be a river was actually a sea stretching almost as wide as the Eastern Ocean.

"Aedan."

Annoyed at his lack of warning, he looked around to find Ashara at the recessed curtained doorway to his inner rooms.

"Yes?"

"The Dogon will grant thee private audience after supper tonight. Thy time is thine own until then. Rasha will escort thee."

He nodded. "Thank you, Ashara."

As unobtrusively as she had come, the Dogon's cousin-wife left his quarters.

Impatience eating at him, Aedan took a step towards that same curtained doorway. The curtains moved again. Aedan suppressed a sigh. Since that first, portentous presentation to the Dogon, he had been treated like a very small child, complete with nursemaid. Told to entertain himself, no word of explanation had been given him as to how—or more importantly, why—he had come to this vast city. On the other hand, Ashara and Rasha and all his other contacts had been eager to answer his questions as long as he confined them to the history and customs of the people about him.

Thus, he had learned that the Dogon was the absolute ruler as well as head of the Ecclesion for the entire Eastern Empire. This filled the east from ocean to ocean—all the world, it seemed, not part of the west. The people who lived in the empire, however, were as diverse as those of the West, but for generation upon generation they had been united into complicated tiers of social, political, and economic classes. Each such status, occupation, tier was indicated by one's clothing, face decoration, language, and residence. Those bright, tattooed faces of his litter bearers, for example, marked the legion of personal soldiers which were attendant upon the Dogon. No wonder the throngs had given way before them when they bore him from the Boatman to the palace.

Aedan thought of the long hours before supper, shrugged, and headed for the door. Somewhere in this maze of interlocking buildings and complexes, a library must exist. Perhaps he could find some answers there before his midnight meeting, for he knew from his short experience in the palace that meals were as elaborately orchestrated as his presentation had been. Course followed course, relieved by interludes of entertainment that ran the gamut from somber choral chants to gyrating, half-naked youths. Midnight would be the earliest that he could expect an audience. It seemed that he was not required to attend upon the Dogon as did his vast, complex retinue.

With a stiff, intricate pattern to his coiffed hair, face powdered white with the metallic green spiral of his station painted upon his left cheek, Rasha grinned as Aedan stepped from his quarters. At a year older than his charge, Rasha was a handsome young man, large-boned but not fat, whose sobering appearance was enlivened by a pair of snapping brown eyes and a mobile mouth often moved to laughter.

"A library?" Rasha's amazement set the vivid spiral insignia on his cheek to movement. "But, of course, my young friend." Brushing an imaginary speck of lint from Aedan's crimson shoulder, Rasha eyed his own resplendent emerald brocade with evident satisfaction as they passed one of the numerous polished brass doors. "And after, maybe you would like to visit the fire-dancers' quarters, eh?"

"Some other time, perhaps," Aedan replied and smiled to soften the blow as he explained. "Ashara tells me I'm to see the Dogon tonight. I'll need all my faculties about me."

Rasha laughed and gestured for Aedan to precede him down another flight of stairs.

"Too true, little one. Tonight...hmm...Mother was quick on your behalf."

"Mother?" Aedan queried. "Ashara is your mother? Then the Dogon is your father? Tell me, then, Rasha—." Aedan's eager questions died as Rasha grinned in mock horror and threw up both hands to halt the flow of questions.

"No, no, no! Yes, Ashara is my mother, but," he continued with an exaggerated look of relief, "the Dogon is not my esteemed father." He shrugged at Aedan's unspoken confusion, guiding him with practiced care through a milling crowd of courtiers and servants, down a further shallow flight of stairs to a second set of doors which gave onto a quiet hall.

"My mother is only a cousin-wife to the Dogon. It is a mark of distinction for my family, you understand, for the Dogon may take as many such wives as he chooses from among the daughters of his father's brothers and his mother's sisters. But his primary wife—she is chosen as he wishes—and she bears the Dogon's heirs.

"No, my mother has her duties to the Dogon, but she was free, then, to choose her own consort—Harpalen, the second overseer of the palace guards." He gestured to the design on his cheek. "I have chosen to follow my father's path. And here," he announced with a flourish, "is the library."

As Aedan was ushered through a rather plain wooden door, he blinked in the sudden dim light, overwhelmed by the cavernous, gloomy vault which stretched before them.

Thousands—no, hundreds of thousands of volumes of all shapes and sizes extended into the gloom which was lifted by small wells of wan light beside uniform tables, stools, and chairs clustered at regular intervals down the center of the space. Where, Aedan wondered with mounting frustration, was he to begin?

"Begin, my dear friend, where you will." Rasha grinned again. "I will visit with the third librarian's second cousin's friend. He is not comely, but his voice is light and his conversation witty."

With that, he led Aedan in the direction of a long-gowned, bearded elder, stooped and thin, who perched on a stool by the first pool of light.

"Dragons, you say?" A dry, wheezing chuckle escaped the old librarian. "Everyone wants to read about dragons. Why not solifluction of upland soils? Or the history and utility of lancing as an accepted medical practice? Dragons, dragons," he muttered under his breath. "Well, come along, young man."

Wheezing along, their progress hindered by the old man's frequent coughing spells, he at last halted Aedan before a series of nested alcoves.

"Here you go. Dragons at your fingertips." The librarian pointed to a small bell on the table before them. "Ring the bell if you require assistance."

Aedan sighed, rubbed a hand through his dark curls, and browsed row after row of books down the line of shelves until a title in his own language caught his attention. *Dragon Sightings in the Western Provinces*, by Eloysia

Tabordottir. The thick volume looked untouched. He pulled the volume free, sneezed at the dust, and carried it over to the table. Taking a seat, he opened a crackling cover to the title page to find that the volume dated more than a hundred years in the past, and then scanned the contents. The book was arranged chronologically and geographically, beginning with the Barrens off the coast of Elfarn to the Naransai Mountains, the Lesser Jihat Peaks of Elfarn, and to the Ma'a'mat Mountains of Mamut. Only the Beyar Mountains between Dravan and Tabor were omitted.

Settling himself at the table, Aedan picked a page at random and read:

During the first interval between the surging of the Dark God's forces and the eventual triumph of the Light, the summer village of Keyash on the landslopes of the Barrens recorded the presence of a dragon in the mountains to the west. A black dragon, it was said to be smallish [i.e., probably not full-grown, E.T.] and came nigh unto the village folk on two occasions....fire ravaged the fields and the inlet, causing that summer's catch to be exceedingly thin....village shaman beseeched the dragon to go away....Curiously, Keyash was spared later when the forces of Da'a came through the region for the villagers had no surplus and that dark army passed them by.

He flipped several pages forward until another passage caught his eye.

Isabeau, Daughter of Light, went unto the Ma'a'mat alone to face the dark god Da'a....She rode to victory and was de-

livered out of those foreboding hills on the back of the red dragon mother, Yltras. This according to one of the lesser books of the Quoran Dru...not convinced of their loyalties, but evidence seems to point to a role against the dark....c.f., a fragment of a folktale from the Halfern side of the Naransai, which tells how the white heart of the dragon Eslevan still draws the light like a beacon of faith into the mountains.

A few minutes after midnight, the Dogon received Aedan in his private chambers. Those gaunt features were remote, but relaxed as the Dogon contemplated the shifting, pulsing colors of a board before him. As he waved his hand across it, the colors flared and receded—shades of blue paling to white, green, giving way to yellow and deep orange and purple-tinged reds. Aedan watched without speaking, curious, until the Dogon lifted his eyes from the patterns created and recreated before him.

"Be seated, little dragon-brother."

At once Aedan knelt upon a cushion across from his host. The Dogon regarded the young man for a long moment—then dropped his eyes back to the colors before him. A slight twist of amusement quirked the corners of his grave eyes as he turned the board to Aedan, who recognized the sinuous coils of a dragon, wings furled at its back.

"Out of the City thou came unto the Boatman and sailed the mighty Dura to the Wall of Flames." The Dogon might have been discussing yesterday's marketing, his voice even, unexcited. "Dost thou know who or what thou art, dragon-brother?"

"I am Aedan Q'tar, son of Mikal the Scholar and Anja—daughter of the light," Aedan replied without hesitation. "My home is...was a small holding on the banks of the River Settern in Halfern, part of the Five Crowns of Aranth."

The Dogon did smile this time. He swept his hand across the board he held and as his hand passed, a map of the world took shape from the colors. He pointed at the map as he spoke.

"The former Five Crowns of Aranth here. The Mamut Empire, so. There, the Southern continent—home to Abri-Hataro and safe from the predations of the West. This, the Eastern Empire, as thou would name it. " One by one the places he indicated sprang to glowing life beneath his fingertips. Yet, as Aedan watched, the heart of the Mamut Empire sucked in the light. Across the Western world, long fingers of black ran, congealed like tar over the map. But, here and there, like prickings of a fire beneath the black, red pinpoints of light poked through, struggled, held. Serene and green, the whole of the Eastern Empire lay free of that dark miasma, as did the Southern continent. Puzzled, Aedan met the Dogon's gaze.

"Thy name—Q'tar—is the title of thy destiny—birthright of the light. Thy mother knew this when thou wert born. *Q'tar*—the gift in a time of dire need—born to be an instrument of power.

"Thou art an empty vessel, boy, meant for the light to flow through thee to send the dark god back to his eternal place of rest in the Ma'a'mat Mountains." The Dogon's voice admitted no doubts. Aedan stared at the Emperor, a shiver of shock and recognition coursing through him as the Dogon's words explained much which had confused him.

"And so I came safely into Abri-Hataro," he mused aloud. "But, why, then, was I allowed to leave the City of Light? Why did no one explain this to me? Unless," he tried to order his whirling thoughts, "it was needful for me to come here, to enlist the aid of the East?"

The Dogon clapped his hands once, sharply. At once, in response to his summons, a delicate-framed, slender woman appeared from some unseen door. On a dark, lacquered stool before the Dogon, she set a tray bearing a flagon, two porcelain cups, a vase holding a tightly furled apricot-colored rosebud, and a single taper. This she lit, bowed low before the Dogon, and then exited without a word. The Dogon took up the flagon from which he poured a golden wine into the cups, offered one to his guest, before taking up one himself. After the first sip, the tension of his pale features eased. Aedan, sipping from his own cup, found that the flavors were complex and delicious.

"Think thou, Aedan Q'tar, that the East would bestir its might for such a foolish piece of business as the ruination of the Five Crowns of Aranth?

"The old King Aranth may turn in his grave, but why should we care? Thy path is thine own to forge, to discover. But, it was foretold long ago that such a one as thou would come. The *Quoran Dru* has guided thy steps at every turning, little dragon-brother. The Lady herself saw and guessed that thou wert not like the others.

"Tell me," the Dogon changed the subject with an abruptness which startled Aedan, "how does thy wine suit?"

"Very well," Aedan answered. He took another sip of the golden liquid.

The Dogon drained his cup, his dark eyes glinting golden in the light of the taper.

"I am the Dogon. Can you understand this much—I was born to rule, to govern, to lead my people. Born into the passage of a tradition so old and so hallowed than Dopan was ancient when the people of the Western world still hunted the kapar and scklear with stone spears and knives!

"I am the keeper of the faith in a line descended from the dragon-gods! Even today, the Dogon drinks the dragon-blood without harm." His deep, mesmerizing voice halted as he took up the small flagon and poured a drop of the wine into the crystal vase that held the apricot-colored rosebud. As the droplet of golden wine met the water, Aedan stared with horrified fascination as the bud blossomed, released its honeyed fragrance, browned, crisped, bent, and fell petal by petal from the once-green stem. With a shaking hand, eyes wide with disbelief, he set his half-empty cup onto the tray.

"Do not fear, Aedan-brother! Hast thou not come through the flames into the dragon-kingdom? Thou art such a one as the West nor East has ever seen before!"

His forefinger stabbed the air before Aedan. "Thy mother knew this. She must have seen the dragon-seed in the heart of thy father, else what drew her love to a simple Halfern man?" He tapped the map in front of him.

"The Western world is threatened by the dark god's forces. But where the Q'tar's name is whispered, hope and rebellion simmer. Thou canst go back, Aedan, and open thy heart to the power of the light and pray that Da'a and his Sindren priests are driven back to the bowels of the Ma'a'mat. Know this: many a Q'tar has perished, though," he conceded with a touch of wry humor, "'tis true the West was succored for a time. Until," his resonant voice deepened, "the dark god's power grew again. It has ever been so, the tides of power shifting back and forth between the light and the dark."

Aedan scowled. The Dogon's wine must be working on him in some way he could not fight. He held his head in his hands. Thus could he see the future unfolding before him—the Five Crowns of Aranth fighting this same battle over and over again. Was there no hope of pushing Da'a back into the depths of the Ma'a'mat and confining his pestilence there forever?

The Dogon stirred.

"Thou could take thy place here, Aedan, like unto another son of the Dogon—for did not the royal court watch as thee drained the dragon's cup? Let the Western world sail on into oblivion."

Aedan shut his eyes tight against his turbulent thoughts. His blood felt as if it boiled and bubbled through his veins. If he opened his mouth, flames might spew forth. If he opened his arms, he might take flight and fly like his dragon-kin before the sun!

His hand unsteady, Aedan covered his cup when the Dogon would have replenished it with more of the wine. The pale ring of flesh on his left hand stood out, bright against the darkly tanned skin.

"Hast thou lost the dragon's stone, then, Aedan Q'tar?" the Dogon demanded of the young man.

Startled, Aedan lifted his gaze from his hand to the hand the Dogon held before him. An emerald-faceted garnet gleamed like a pulsing heartbeat on the older man's left hand. No, he thought in confusion, he hadn't lost his father's ring. He'd put it somewhere, somewhere.... He couldn't think clearly. Mesmerized, Aedan stared into that garnet so like a pool of dark-red water. Like a river, he thought, it flowed powerful and steady, carrying him along. Almost he might have been swept along the familiar banks of the Settern to step ashore at a sturdy, well-built pier. Striding along a wide graveled path, he came up through the river meadows to find the holding winding down the day. Home! Smoke drifted from the chimneys, the last sinking rays of sun reflected orange and violet from the keeping room windows. His pace quickening now, he shoved the door open. *She* heard his step, unguarded and impatient as he'd come—and she danced across the floor to greet him, light and quick and glad, blue eyes smiling and blonde hair escaping its long, loose braid....

Aedan came to himself with a start, conscious of time having passed. Across the room, he saw the Dogon splashing water on his face as an attendant held fresh robes. Daylight softened the man's harsh, brooding features. Putting out a cautious hand to steady himself, Aedan sat up on the cushions on which he'd slept, but if he thought the wine he'd drunk the night before would set his head to spinning, he discovered just the opposite. He felt clear-headed, his course of action acknowledged and accepted.

The Dogon slipped into his garments, his attendant replaced by another one laden with a tray of new breads and freshly brewed tea. Aedan's stomach growled and the dragon-king chuckled.

"So, little brother, I trust thy rest proved refreshing?" He did not wait for a reply, but poured out two cups of steaming, fragrant tea, and took up one of the light, sweet breads that came in innumerable shapes and flavors. "Cleanse thyself, little brother," the Dogon indicated the attendants who appeared with more water and raiment that he recognized as his own. "Then thou may tell me how thou hast decided to turn thy back on the Dragon-Kingdom!"

The Dogon sipped his tea on the small, private balcony that overlooked both the palace complex and the city of Dopan below. Aedan joined him and together they surveyed the vast, sprawling urban center already alight with movement and life as markets were made ready and artisans loosened the awnings of their workshops.

"Every drop of blood in my veins responds to the rhythms of this city." The Dogon gestured to the view below. "Do not think me walled off in isolation from my people and their lives, I am as much a part of their world as thee within thy holding. Heart and home, eh, my dragon-brother?"

Aedan nodded. That vision which had come to him in the heart of the garnet—a dream brought on by that extraordinary wine. But, just as certainly, he knew that his future was tied to Halfern and holding—yes, indeed, heart and home. The Dogon's soft sleeve brushed the flesh of Aedan's bare hand as he clasped the young man by the shoulder.

"We are truly kin, young Aedan. Born of the dragon's seed. How this is so, I do not know. But, wherever thou should roam, remember that the power of the dragon is thine to draw upon." He quoted, assuring Aedan, "Here, indeed, is proof, my young doubter:

Sun-fired, those born of the dragon
Fly wind-fierce, loosed by the might of dawn
To wield the light against the dark god
And his soulless minions! Dragon-seed,
Thy wings await thee! This is the sixth
Observation of the Quoran Dru.

"Fly, little dragon-brother, where thou wilt. Thou could rule the entire world, if it were thy will. But," the Dogon pressed Aedan's shoulder, "it must be thy will."

"I don't understand," Aedan lifted bewildered eyes to his companion. "Any of this. I thought dragons were legends, stories told to children." He waited but the Dogon did not protest that such creatures yet lived. He went on. "I've never had any strange powers. Only a sickness as I came of age and that has passed."

The Dogon pulled Aedan by the arm and led him to a pool of water that graced the terraced balcony, reflecting the dancing rays of morning light.

"Spread thy wings, Aedan Q'tar," the Dogon commanded from behind him in a voice which rang with undercurrents of excitement. Without thought or hesitation, Aedan complied, lifting his arms straight out to his sides. The faintest flow of air surged beneath his outstretched arms, as though he might push off with his toes and rise on the warming, rising air currents.

"Close thine eyes," the Dogon whispered behind him, "then tell me what thou can see on the Dogon's ship that comes even now into the far side of the harbor."

Like a soaring seabird, or a dragon, Aedan thought, he felt as if he were skimming over rooftops and city streets, then over open water. The black-masted sloop carried one lithe figure—a dark-haired, dark-eyed woman who lifted gleaming eyes of recognition to him as he passed above her. Her long slim fingers traced the curves of the Dogon's symbol in the air before her. Then he opened his eyes on the Dogon's balcony and described the woman.

"Thy dragon-sister, my daughter, Aleisha."

Aedan spun about, eyed the older man, whose gaunt features seemed more focused and stronger than any face he'd ever known before.

"I looked upon that ship!" He gestured with a shaking hand to the tiny speck of movement that marked the harbor entrance, "but I never really left here, did I?

The Dogon shrugged.

"It was not necessary. If 'tis thy will, Aedan, thou canst ride the light like the son of the dragon. The dragons' promise is eternal, their strength unflagging, and their hearts unquenchable! Remember this and let my words be thy guide."

Rasha stepped onto the balcony with the dark-haired woman from the ship. Aedan gaped in spite of himself, and Aleisha smiled as she embraced her father.

"The ship is prepared, Father. Is he ready?"

The Dogon looked at Aedan, one brow raised. For answer, Aedan reached out his hands to his dragon-kin.

Chapter 12

"He will not eat, Holy One."

The seated, robed figure with a hood shadowing all of his features except for his eyes never moved, but the man at the window made a slight movement as of impatience or sudden anger. The tiny scarlet star in his ear caught the sun as he smoothed the gold buttons on his heavy, plain coat with tapering, elegant fingers—unused, the acolyte noted with contempt, to any hard labor. The dark, ascetic features frowned, and the man's dark eyes dilated as if some wholly unpleasant thought occurred to him. Quickly, the acolyte averted his eyes from the visitor and shifted his gaze back to the silent figure before him. The gloom and chill of the room seeped into his bony feet, drawing the meager warmth from his thin legs.

"He tests us," said the voice from beneath the hood.

"He must not die!" The man by the window turned away from the window to address the hooded one. "We snared but half a fish, Holy One. With this one as bait, we shall have the other half in our hands." The intensity of his voice jarred at the young stubbled acolyte. In his short service to the Corps, he had already seen scores of such prisoners meet a death that came too late for mercy. Why should this one matter so much?"

A dismissive glance passed between the hooded one and his visitor. A barely perceptible nod indicated the acolyte.

"The prisoner shall be moved to the infirmary. See to it, son of Da'a."

"At thy will, Holy One."

The young messenger bowed to the blood-red eye of Da'a that adorned the hand extended before him, shuffled to the door and made sure it was fully closed behind him. How, the brief thought crossed his mind, had this one prisoner deserved such a reprieve? Then he dismissed the stray thought and hurried down a twisting side stair to the courtyard. With a shudder he crossed to the prison quarters. Above the dungeons the smoke of the crematory drifted like an accusing finger—death to the enemies of Da'a!"

Stroking Kapura's damp curls, Isman-Bati settled the feverish child in his lap as Ashrat-F'tor pressed firm fingers against the glands in her neck.

"F'tor-bani," the doctor addressed his moon-faced assistant in a soft, melodious voice, "if thou wouldst. Tirsan tea, not too strong, sweetened."

The assistant opened the woven case he held and withdrew a crackling paper tied with a green thread. His black eyes met those of Isman with a serene confidence. Nodding to master and worried father, F'tor-bani moved with a grace belying his rotund figure for all of his weight, towards Mari-Isman's open kitchen.

Ashrat's cool gaze followed the short, receding figure of the bani, then he straightened.

"This little one will sleep well and wake better, Isman. The tea will bring her fever down. As to the other," his voice did not change as he continued, "he is in worse shape than his fellows. He has refused his food for days now. The Sindren leader, Chabal V'na himself, has ordered him taken to the infirmary."

Isman waited. Ashrat shrugged as the bani reappeared at the other end of the courtyard, Mari-Isman and a sub-dued Sherat flanking him.

"It remains to be seen whether he shall live."

The physician lifted Kapura's unresisting body from her father's arms and cradled her against his broad chest, taking the steaming cup from the tray proffered by the bani. "Drink, little one. Ashrat will help thee."

F'tor-bani, busy with his packets behind his master, never noticed that the latter of Ashrat's words were directed to the father and not to the child he held. Isman-Bati reached for his wife's hand. Two sets of black eyes gleamed as the cloth merchant and Mari-Isman inclined their heads in brief thanks. Ashrat soft voice crooned to the child as Kapura's bright eyes closed.

Weighted in darkness, Barak held fast to the certainty that his comrades lived and that Aedan was not taken by the Sindren. Secure in that knowledge, death held no fear for him. He lay on the floor of his fetid cell and fell at last into a deep and dreamless sleep.

It was the absence of the cold, the pain, which roused him. Without opening his eyes or changing position, not yet fully conscious, he heard sounds, saw light beneath his lids, and guessed with a wry note of satisfaction that his hunger strike had at last succeeded in provoking a re-action from his captors. Time enough, he decided as he slid fast towards sleep again, to wake later.

The evening sun rode low in the sky, as turquoise and violet and orange-suffused clouds spread and moved along the western horizon. On a dusty rooftop overlook-ing the Sindren complex, two pigeons roosted on the cor-nice, cooing and rustling as they settled to quiet. Like a part of the structure of the roof, Obal lay unmoving be-neath a dust-covered tarpaulin and trained his seeking lens past the roosting pigeons to the compound beyond. For three days now, he had crawled into position in the afternoon, relieving Assir, storing away the details of the daily regimen within the Corps' quarters.

Shifting his gaze a fraction to the left, he swept the lens across the scene below. This slow, methodical sweep had occurred over and over as he watched. The original purpose of the Sindren compound had been to serve as diplomatic headquarters for Mamut trading delegations. Behind the walled exterior and to the right lay the quar-ters for the priests' garrison. To the left of the gate lay the messenger dogs' barracks. Beyond the garrison stood the stark, closed building which housed the priestly elite, headed by Chabal V'na. Da'a's own temple, hastily constructed when the compound was converted, adjoined this building on a diagonal. Behind the temple and forming the far wall was the warren of rooms assigned to the acolytes and lesser priests.

Next to the dogs' quarters, across the courtyard, lay the stables set into the west wall. Ranged along this wall to the north was the complex of outbuildings housing the kitchens, storerooms, and infirmary. And there, in the corner, the Sindren prison cells and dungeon rose adjacent to the small round building with its central smokestack—the crematory. Obal suppressed a shudder. The smoke had been stilled—until today. His big knuckles tightened. By the Light! Were they too late?

Scratching his mount between the ears as the stallion nuzzled at his open palm, Caskar fretted with an outward show of calm. With Dunkil riding back to Tabor, he nursed his secret and his rising impatience alone. Worse, he had noticed one of the anonymous, sweaty-palmed lesser priests following him at a distance on his last visit to the morning market in the Lower City of Altari-Maro.

Shifting his stance to widen his view of the compound, he took in the small group traversing the central courtyard between the Temple of Da'a and Chabal V'na's quarters. There, at the elbow of Chabal V'na himself, paced a mute, robed figure—a pious visitor from one of the provinces and an important one at that to be accorded so close a position to the temple leader. The gaunt figure struck a nerve with the young Halfern dog—that controlled stride, restrained power in the tensed lines of the body beneath the robe. Where had he seen such a man before? Surely not in the temple complex. Then where? Home in Halfern?

His eyes narrowing, Caskar took an involuntary step back. His stallion nudged him. When he was younger, yes! Just a schoolboy running with his playmates in the village square. The man with the closed face and dour mood, for whom not even Aedan could hide his dislike. The man who shouted in anger at the village children, cursed them, and kicked at them like vermin if they crossed his path. Zaavan! Zaavan, the traitor!

Here, in Altari-Maro! To question the Sindren prisoner? The little companion of the giant Obal? Caskar's fingers tightened in the forelock of his horse. The stallion moved against him as it caught that sudden flood of panic. A trap? Obal must be warned. Chabal V'na held the little Halfern man to lure Obal and the others from hiding. But, the desperate thought beat at him, how could he warn them when he himself was being watched?

As if the very thought bore fruit, the hooded visitor raised his head, his glance sweeping the courtyard. With alacrity, the Halfern dog tucked himself further into the shadows and stilled his restless stallion with a reassuring pat. Zaavan's eyes raked the open stable doors, but he did not pause. Caskar let out his pent-up breath with a sigh as the temple leader's party mounted the steps to Chabal V'na's quarters and disappeared inside.

Even cloistered alone with Zaavan, the rest of the Sindren enclave shut out, Chabal V'na's words came disembodied from the depths of his cowl. Only the shadowed eyes—flaring points of light like the eyes of Da'a himself—and the hands—long-fingered, never stilled—were revealed.

"Come, Zaavan, sit," Chabal V'na's hand pointed to a chair near the fire burning in the center of the room. "Some wine, if you will." Another slight gesture motioned to the chased silver carafe to hand on a table between the chairs.

Hiding a sense of uneasiness, Zaavan poured a goblet for the temple leader and for himself before taking the seat indicated and waited. Encounters with Chabal V'na were never purely social.

"How sits the power of Da'a in Halfern, Zaavan? Do the peasants grow used to His Presence and His Power?"

Startled, Zaavan threw a sharp glance at the hooded high priest. Was that a mocking note he heard?

"They are ignorant, Holy One. But they bow to His Presence and His Power."

"For the love of Da'a, my lord Zaavan, or for the saber?"

Again, that odd note seemed to color Chabal V'na's words. Perhaps a trick of the cowl? The truth, he decided as he took a sip of his wine.

"Mostly for the saber, Holy One. Yet, it has stilled their grumbling and filled the temple plate. And the hands of Da'a spread out to welcome ever more hopefuls drawn to His Might."

"Spoken like a true son of Da'a!"

This time there was no mistaking the temple leader's mockery. Stung, Zaavan replied, the red star dancing in his ear as he faced the Sindren high priest.

"Do you doubt me, Holy One?"

A deep cackle of laughter, distorted through the hood, shook Chabal V'na. Tapping his fingertips together, he waited until the slow flush of red receded from Zaavan's contorted features.

"I doubt you, Zaavan, in this one thing—your desire to have this Halfern youngling brought home to the temple, home to his salvation, home to Da'a—mightiest lord of eternity!"

Shaken, Zaavan dropped his head in a gesture of submission and chose his words with studied care before he answered the challenge.

"I am weak, Holy One!" His hooded eyes turned to the man beside him. "My vanity was wounded when the boy slipped from my hands, and yes, even earlier when he was led astray from the path to Da'a by his most unholy parents and his heathen companions.

"Yet, I swear to you, I struggle daily against my sins. This child must be brought to Da'a! If he is truly the one we seek, Holy One, then he will provide such a tool for Da'a, against the likes of which none shall be spared!"

Chabal V'na held up a hand.

"Calm yourself, Zaavan. Your fervor overwhelms me. Know that we shall have this boy brought to Da'a. I wish only to remind you where your loyalties are bound." He paused, sipping his wine, giving the warning time to sink in. "Now, to matters at hand. Why should I not feed this infidel Halfern man who lies witless in the infirmary to the fires of the mouth of Da'a?"

Zaavan drained his goblet before responding, giving himself cover to think through his argument for saving the prisoner.

"Because, Holy One, that one is never separated from his companion. The two of them spirited the boy away from the holding. Catch the other and we will have the boy."

"How," Chabal V'na questioned, his tone harsh and accusatory, "is it that no sign of this boy has been seen in the city? Where could he hide that we should not see him before this?"

"My lord," the red star glinted as a faint sheen of sweat glistened high on Zaavan's cheeks, 'it may be that he has been hidden beyond the city since one of them was captured. But," cold certainty rang in his voice, "the other will know where to find him. The one we have shall bring us to his companion. Then we shall have Aedan Q'tar in the hands of Da'a."

"Hmm." The cowled head shifted to face his guest. "Two days, Zaavan, then—." The temple leader turned with a hiss as the door to the chamber swung open after a hasty knock. One of the smooth-shaven elder priests bent a knee in the direction of his superior, who barked, "Yes, Telsit? What is it?"

"A Dravanian dog from the Laltepoch cell has arrived, Holy One, with a message bearing the seal of Da'a."

"Send him in at once!"

Zaavan's brow rose with unconcealed curiosity. The seal of Da'a! A message meant for the Holy One's eyes only. A broken seal meant the death of the dog.

A small, dark man, his compact figure radiating extreme fatigue and the smell of the saddle, followed Telsit in and sank to his knees before the hooded Sindren priest. From his tunic he drew a creased brown parchment, folded and sealed with the grimacing red image of Da'a. A visible wave of relief sagged the taut shoulders of the dog as the seal passed the temple leader's inspection.

Chabal V'na, Zaavan noticed with well-hidden contempt, could not resist the momentary torture of this insignificant messenger by lingering over his inspection of the seal.

"To the barracks with him, Telsit." Chabal V'na jabbed a finger at the sagging figure of the dog. Telsit gestured at the open doorway and two blank-faced acolytes stepped into the room. Half-dragging the Dravanian rider, they removed him from the chamber. Telsit followed them out, closing the door to the chamber behind him.

Chabal V'na snapped the seal, shook out the folds of the parchment. The dark hood was unmoving as he read the message. Then in one convulsive movement, the high priest's fingers clenched and crumpled the parchment, which he tossed into the flames of the firepit before them.

"They dare!" Chabal V'na cried. He jerked about to confront Zaavan, who shifted in his seat in spite of himself. "The rebellious population dares to defy the will of Da'a! Oh," he noted with a sardonic laugh as Zaavan's eyes widened with alarm, "it is only insignificant acts of defiance. High priest Gagues closes in on the perpetrators even as we speak.

"But he writes that these petty acts are fueled by the rabble's belief in the rise of some son of the light!" A grating, disdainful laugh shook the Sindren priest. He pointed at Zaavan's face with a long, bony finger. "Your work! It can only be word of this boy—this child you let slip away. He must be found and brought to me!" There was no mistaking the emphasis in Chabal V'na's words. He meant to have Aedan in his power.

"Yes, Holy One!" Zaavan bowed his head over a deeply bent knee before the angry cowled figure of the high priest. "It shall be done as you command!" Rising, he backed out the chamber, pulling the door closed as he went, his countenance veiled to the lurking Telsit.

Striding through the corridor and down the stairs to the hallway that would take him to his own chamber, he nursed his private thoughts away from prying eyes. Aedan would be found! But the boy would yield up the secret of his power to Zaavan! Yes, he wore the yoke of the Sindren god only in this much—in that it brought him closer and closer to the power he sought, had always sought. Even in the holding, with the dark-haired witch of the light. From the moment he had sensed a different kind of power, he had known where his destiny lay. Far, far beyond the beret's nest that was the holding! Reaching his chamber, he thrust open the door of his chamber and locked it behind him. Somehow, the Halfern brat would be his key to power.

Testing the taut rope, Obal hoisted Assir up to get a good grip well above his head. Shavi, his swarthy features likewise swaddled in a Sindren robe and hood, went up the rope after the young man. Hand over hand, silent as shadows, the two figures ascended the wall, reached the top, and rolled over flat into the darkness beyond. When three spaced tugs pulled at the rope in his hands, Obal attached a second rope, paid it out slowly, and watched it disappear up the wall.

What, he wondered with growing impatience, was keeping Isman-Bati? The night was still. Little of the night-time bustle of the Lower City reached this block. Small wonder if Altari-Maro's inhabitants gave the Sindren cell a wide berth. From inside the compound came the muted sounds of the Sindren evening services. Good! Those within the walls were undisturbed in the halls of Da'a. Now, if only Isman-Bati would get on with his part in this night's work!

Pop! Pop! Pop! Down below in the Lower City, green sprays of light shot straight up into the liquid blackness of the star-filled sky. Sparks cascaded and showered over the general area of the harbor and its crowded warehouses. The acrid smell of smoke had barely reached him when he heard running feet on the street before the compound and a startled, high-pitched query from the Sindren sentries.

Moments later, shouts rang out within, and the chanting halted. The sharp swearing of jostling priests and the excited whickers from the horses came to him, then the pounding of riders and foot-priests. The rope twitched in his hands. Settling himself, Obal followed his comrades over the wall into the Sindren complex. He spared a swift prayer that the cloth merchant, having started a fire in the Sindren warehouses, would be as effective at hindering efforts to douse it. The trick, of course, was to keep the Corpsmen occupied for as long as possible.

Making greater speed now, Obal landed on the inside of the wall. Assir and Shavi made for the dungeons, seeking those prisoners still held in isolation cells, while he set off in the deepest shadows for the infirmary. Dressed as Sindren priests, his two comrades must depend on the Light to guide them to their friends. He, on the other hand, could not hope to pass as such.

The rough, white-washed wall of the infirmary caught at his beard as he edged with cautious step around a corner. A thin square of wan light spilled from the arch of a recessed doorway. Scuttling like a zantling crab, Obal slipped inside. Cheap tallow candles marked the entrance, and, inside, the room with its single line of cots was lit by dim sconces, as if the Corps were not prepared to provide decent light for those who came sick to the infirmary. Only one cot, at the far end of the room, was occupied that night. Obal scanned the interior of the room before moving further into the space. Shelves with spikes of dried herbs and plants and crockery and closed cupboards took up one entire wall opposite the cots. Narrow shuttered closets flanked the four corners of the room.

Another recessed door stood open a crack at the other end of the room. Private quarters for the attendants? Surely a keeper must be on duty within. Something about the set-up stirred a restless tendril of caution in Obal and he stepped back against the entrance door. Maybe best to reconnoiter outside again? Yet, the sight of Barak's limp body, one skeletal arm resting on the sheet covering him, made the big man throw caution to the wind and sidle into the room.

Behind him he was aware of shutters flung open and half-turning, saw a lieber-saber aiming as he swung low, diving for his assailant's knees. The Sindren Corpsman was nearly a match for him in size. Together they grappled and cursed, rolling over to crash against a cot. Unable to loosen his grip on the hand wielding the lieber-saber, Obal found himself taking a beating along the side of his face as his attacker attempted to bash him unconscious. One more minute, one more minute, and he just might succeed.

A sharp snapping sound whipped in the air above them. The Sindren Corpsman fell limp against Obal, the lieber-saber rolling from his hand. A rustling came from the room beyond. Rolling over, Obal pushed the body of the Sindren priest away, and peered above the cot. A slight figure dropped the metal chamber pot he held and bent to retrieve the lieber-saber. Obal lumbered to his feet. Caskar grinned, then sobered, his white face averted from the bleeding priest.

"Take Barak quickly! Zaavan waits for you!"

The Halfern giant stopped in mid-stride, his breath coming in gasps.

"Zaavan!" The murderous whisper froze Caskar's blood. "Here?"

"No, Obal!" Caskar hurried around him, stripped the sheet from Barak and fumbled with a robe about the still figure. As Obal turned about, his gaze blood-red and set, the young dog grasped at his sleeve, begging. "Help me, Obal! I can't save Barak or the Q'tar by myself. Obal, time is running out!"

Half-dragging the pleading Caskar with him, Obal swung about again, conflicting desires plain upon his face. Then his sight focused on the thin heap of robe that was his friend. Without a word, he picked up that near-weightless bundle and headed for the door. At the wall they found Assir steadying a swaying figure as Shavi pulled up the rope. Caskar helped tie Barak into a similar harness on the second rope, speaking in a rapid undertone to Obal.

"I saw him. Yesterday. With Chabal V'na, the temple leader. They're watching me, Obal. I couldn't get word. I waited and watched. Tonight, with the sudden commotion, I thought perhaps you'd come. I went to the infirmary, through the back. The young acolyte within never saw me. I didn't hit him hard." The tense, white face blurred as Caskar bit his lip, looked away. "Then I cracked the door to the sickroom and waited some more. Then you came." He sniffed once. "I didn't know the other fellow was hiding in that cupboard until he burst out after you."

"You saved my life. And his." Obal nodded at Barak's bundled body as he was lifted up the wall. "And Aedan's. Come with us now," the big man urged the young man.

"How can I? If I go, they'll know. My sisters...."

Obal gave a harsh sigh.

"Then needs must, I think, keep you from harm as best we may. I'm sorry, young Caskar."

Obal's right fist flashed, tapped, and Caskar sagged over a massive shoulder as the Halfern giant bent to catch the young man's body. Slipping through the shadows, he made his way to the dogs' stables and eased his burden to the ground before a stall that bore the Halfern crest. Undoing the stable doors to the mounts of the remaining dogs, Obal hied the horses towards the open stable doors away from the small body of his countryman. Let it appear as if the boy had been trying to save his mount.

For one agonizing moment he stared into the night towards the central block of buildings that must hold Chabal V'na's quarters. Zaavan! So close! And after, came the thought of Aedan. With a last check to make sure that Caskar was out of harm's way, Obal faded into the darkness, gained the wall without obstruction, and tugged at the rope to give warning of his ascent.

Chapter 13

Ashrat and Obal flanked the cot where Barak rested. An empty bowl testified to the little man's returning hunger. But when Ashrat lifted the mug of steaming tea—an herbal concoction to help one sleep—Barak grimaced, pushed it aside, and groped for Obal's hand.

"The seeking." He drew himself up from the pillow upon which he rested as Obal stared in blank comprehension at his companion. "The seeking," Barak insisted.

Isman-Bati stepped forward from his position at the foot of the cot, motioned to Ashrat to wait.

"The hollow, friend-Barak. What we attempted there, yes?"

With a sigh of relief, Barak fell back upon his pillow.

"That woman!" Obal's outrage had not lessened.

"Wait," the cloth merchant held up a hand, admonishing his friend. Obal bit his lip and scowled.

"You saw something during the seeking?"

Barak's eyes lit up. He nodded. "The lashings." He lay silent for a minute, gathering breath and energy to speak. "Halstav." His voice came as a bare pattern of sound above his labored breathing, and he did not resist this time as Ashrat held the cup to his mouth.

As his friend slipped into sleep, his breathing eased. Obal lingered a moment before following Ashrat and Isman-Bati from the shadowed, cool room. The three men stood on the upper verandah above Isman's courtyard. Muffled voices reached them, attesting to the presence of the children elsewhere in the abode. Only Assir sat below in close conference with a demure, sloe-eyed daughter of a neighbor. The girl's mother and Mari-Isman could be seen seated behind a screen. Light flashed about the girl's soft, contoured features as she dipped and raised her chin in response to Assir's low-voiced conversation.

Isman smiled as Assir looked up, saw his father on the verandah, and nodded before turning his attention back to his guest.

"Well, friend-Obal? Does Halstav hold any meaning for you?"

Obal stroked his beard before replying.

"Halstav is a Halfern port, Isman. I know no more of it than that. Barak and I spent a short time amongst the petty holdings that carve up the plain about the port, long before we ever came to Mikal the Scholar's holding." A long sigh escaped him. "But I don't recall any weavings or such like."

"Perhaps a ship that caught his eye in the harbor?" Ashrat offered.

Obal shrugged in bafflement.

The three men made their way down into a corner of the courtyard and settled at a small table set in the shadows of a palm. As if waiting for their father, Joghar and

Bahri appeared with trays of tea and delicate pastries. When Isman had shooed his youngest two away, he turned to Obal.

"Think my friend," the cloth merchant urged. "You must have seen, else Barak would have tried to tell us more."

Frustrated, Obal balled his great hands into helpless fists.

"Come," Isman encouraged him. "Drink your tea. Tell me," he flicked a brief, amused glance at the big Halfern rover, "how big is this port? I've always thought of Halfern as a sedate land of farmers and holdings. What kept two adventurers such as Barak and yourself in Halstav?"

A low rumble of sheepish laughter erupted from his companion.

"This dancer." Obal shot a bawdy glance at Isman and Ashrat, his hands tracing her curves in the air. "Barak thought she favored him. We drank and gambled and paid the dancer for her company. Old Po-twee's place, it was."

"On the waterfront?"

"Of course." Obal shook his head. "The place was always full of sailors. Almeridian *dabois*—like monkeys they were, climbing the rigging of those tall-masted sloops. Fight at the drop of a hat, sometimes for a single coin!"

"Dravanians, too, I bet," Isman put in, encouraging the flow of reminiscences.

"Ho!" Obal slapped his thigh and roared with laughter. "Quick those Dravanians were with the knives! Knick a man before he knew what he was about! But," he allowed, "the best drinking companions to be found on land or water." He finished his tea.

"I remember once when old Po-twee's one-eyed wife bet a Dravanian sub-cap'n he couldn't outdrink her—shot for shot of that rotgut tuber-spirit that passes for drink in Dravan."

Isman murmured in appreciation and held up a hand as Ashrat opened his mouth.

"Well, Saquatl—that was the sub-cap'n—he downed about a half-dozen shots and was fading fast. A couple of sailors from some other ship, seeing the way the game was going, tried to muscle in on the bet and up the ante on old Po-twee's better half.

"Stupid beggars! Never tangled with a half-drunk Dravanian and his knives before!"

"Not to mention," Isman interjected with a sly glance, "two half-drunk Halfern wayfarers."

Obal roared with laughter.

"We tore up old Po-twee's place kind of rough, then chased those black-tunicked water rats right back to their ship. What a fight that was!"

"And their ship?" Isman slipped his question deftly into Obal's train of thought.

"Oh, she was an odd one, all right. Low-slung, oared and masted. Swift in the water, for sure. And little room for cargo, as I recall." He turned to the Altari-Maro merchant. "We thought then p'rhaps she had other business in port. Yes, indeed...." He stopped short, stared hard at Isman.

"She was an Easten ship, black-masted. Funny thing, too, how all her rigging was twined and lashed together—like it could give and hold with every wave or storm that came its way."

"Look now, Obal," Isman pointed out, "you do remember."

"By the Light!" Obal swore, his eyes huge with amazement. "If the lad's shipped on an Eastern sloop!" He could not continue, his shoulders slumping.

The cloth merchant touched his friend's arm.

"Such come here, as you have seen—for trade and other business. I have even been to the trading enclave at Aeopar. Perhaps we can glean some useful information from my contacts there."

"But," Obal's face sagged, "how much longer? How will we ever find Aedan?"

"Time," Isman soothed, "it will take time to arrange, but in the meantime, our friend Barak will rest and heal, yes?"

Obal's features brightened. He grinned.

"At least if he's in the East, Aedan will be free from these whey-faced Sindren rakar-snakes!"

Fussing with the heavy black curtains, Zaavan grunted with satisfaction as the room sank into absolute darkness, save for the single candle that strove to cast its wan light in the center of the cell. The cell was one of several private altars reserved for the pilgrims who came bearing gifts for Da'a. No one would notice anything amiss in his use of such a cell at any hour he chose.

The candle sat upon a concave porphyritic altar stone that stood alone in the heart of the space. On the wall opposite the curtained doorway, the polished mask of Da'a stretched from floor to ceiling. Zaavan barely glanced at the god-mask, dismissing the thin, cruel features drawn back in the caricature of a welcoming smile. The wide, deep-set eyes seemed to devour the unwary, so that Zaavan never met them if possible. The skull, smooth and elongated, suggested an intelligence, a depth of cunning and control that was well-echoed in his servant Chabal V'na, Zaavan reflected. The ears lay pinned back, almost like an animal's, but there—on the right lobe—was the old scar Da'a had received in battle against his mortal enemies. There the light had marked him with a curious pattern, much like the red star that dangled from his own right earlobe.

Now, all was in readiness. The dark god would let loose his power through Zaavan and—soon—through his instrument, the Halfern stripling. He bit down the anger that he had so far failed to regain the boy, Aedan. But now, now the girl was his last hope—his last tie—to his elusive prey. He eased the cloth away to uncover the blood-red stone. The candle's flame seemed to expand as the garnet caught the light. Once the ring in which it was set had gleamed on the finger of that Halfern witch Anja who had spurned his advances. Even now he gloated, remembering how she had suffered. Da'a had answered his prayers and brought a pestilence upon her. That had driven her to seek the mountains and her death.

But, he had seen the ring Anja had worn entrusted to the boy's wet-nurse. Seen and known it to be somehow connected to her power. Biding his time, he waited for the power to be manifest in the boy. But then had come his banishment from the holding, the death of that fool, Mikal, and the unmistakable evidence that the boy possessed something of his mother's power. Thus had he consolidated his position with timely gifts to the Sindren leadership and returned to the holding. Gagues had played no small part in aiding him. When the boy was spirited away, he had recalled the ring the old nursemaid held. The boy wore a like ring—his father's. He had guessed that one could lead him to the other.

However, something had happened. This ring had shown him not the boy, Aedan, but a girl. It seemed that she too was searching for the boy. Her position changed from day to day. Gagues had been less than successful in trapping her, but had sent a private message through the Dravanian dog. She seemed to be heading ever eastward, and if she ever came nigh unto the holding, he would have her! Failing that, if she came over the Naransai mountains like the boy before her, she would be driven straight into his clutches. But now he needed time. Gagues was easily handled, but Chabal V'na was another matter. Rather, the cold thought came to Zaavan, like waking to find a rakar snake coiled on one's pillow.

Zaavan focused on the garnet. The candle flame hesitated, then went out as he blew upon it. The dark red stone glowed yet before the mask of Da'a. Cold, scarlet fingers of light traced the features of the dark god. The pitiless, remote face seemed to kindle to life, watching as Zaavan concentrated his total awareness upon the gleaming heart of the garnet.

Good, he thought. She slept. Her thin body was taut, ready for flight even in sleep. He projected himself into her thoughts. '*Come, child, come to safety! Let me help you! Come, come!*' She stirred, restless now as she reacted to his words. '*Let me come to you, child! Show me the way!*' Over and over, Zaavan strained to impress that illusion of comfort upon her sleeping mind. Again she tossed, whimpered. '*Poor lost daughter,*' he crooned, '*trust in me.*' Her mind began to relax, loosen its control. Then, a dark hand shook the girl. No! She was coming back to wakefulness. No! No!

Zaavan sucked in his breath in sharp disappointment. So close! He raised his eyes to the mask of Da'a where the blood-red light faded away. Tomorrow the Dravanian dog would ride for home. He would contrive to send a message to Gagues. Perhaps if he raised the stakes? Chabal V'na would exact a swift revenge if he had the slightest suspicion that Gagues acted from personal motives!

Keeping his ears alert and his eyes on the bowl of stew before him, Caskar listened to the talk running up and down the tables around him. Several new dogs had ridden into the Sindren compound over the past few days. A new one from Tabor, too. This was a thin, taciturn man in his late twenties. A scar twisted about the back of his hand as he raised his tankard. His presence worried Caskar. What

had happened to Dunkil? But others, including the little swarthy Dravanian Uxpal and a coarse-haired Elfarn
woman with a mustache on her upper lip, were also recent
arrivals. Why all this attention focused on Altari-Maro,
the young man mused. Everyone knew that Chabal V'na
sat on the right-hand side of the Mamut Emperor, but
why all these messengers at once? Across the table, the
Tabor man spoke in a soft voice to his neighbor. Caskar
strained to hear, draining off a sip from his mug of weak
ale.

"Trouble... between the lakes and the Naransai...."

His companion kept his comments low, then the Tabor
dog replied, shaking his head.

"No, not that direction. The Aleri were involved. I
heard," he lowered his voice even further, casting a bright,
furtive glance about him, "that a village massacred a
whole party of *them*—camped outside the village. No
doubt about their intentions!"

"Aleri!" The second dog's voice was incredulous. "*They*
must have been mad! Why would anyone attack the fisherfolk?"

The general hubbub and bustle increased as weary or
bored messengers finished their meal, others arriving to
take their places at the trencher tables. Caskar missed the
thread of the Tabor rider's conversation, and then his ears
pricked as a snort of laughter choked the Almeridian who
listened as closely next to the Tabor dog.

"Hat'm Sin! Go on, Bazin!"

"It's true," Bazin insisted with a short grin, wiping the foaming ale from his upper lip. "I saw him myself, hopping up and down like a black toad and just as poisonous with his eyes and belly bulging! Dafydd was a prize catch. Someone slipped up there!"

"Got clean away, eh? Then...."

No need to finish that thought, Caskar thought with glee. They all knew one another, the Emperor's dogs. With her hostage escaped, Dunkil was free to make good her own escape from the Mamut emperor's service. No doubt she was even now reunited with her blind healer of a brother.

Quan Matar's long body was hunched over the drooping ears of his sad-faced donkey. They made an admirable pair. Ahead of him, Jani's mount made a sudden lurch towards a thicket of veldt-berry bushes. Farther ahead, Nepentha's tall, straight-backed form swayed upon a sure-footed pony that would not dare step off the trail that wound in a precarious fashion along the outer slopes of Wassen Tor in the midst of the Naransai range. They were making good time on their trek to Taavel, for Nepentha was persuaded that the clue to the Q'tar's present whereabouts must lay at his point of disappearance. The seer, Carrig, would be their contact. Quan Matar's donkey balked out of the blue, braying to wake the dead. Jani looked back, her eyes wide with surprise which turned to alarm.

"Hold!"

The imperious command rang before and behind them as a rough-clad group surrounded their small party. Quan Matar untangled his long legs from his donkey as Nepentha halted and stood her ground. The granary clerk shrugged as he caught Jani's glance, then pulled his unprotesting donkey along to Jani's side. With mounting apprehension, he surveyed the silent advancement of their captors.

A thin, russet-haired woman, her features hard as the red rocks of Wassen Tor, approached Nepentha. The tailor's daughter sat her pony tight-lipped, Quan Matar observed, although the tautness of her shoulders portrayed her mounting fury.

"State your business, woman-of-the-city," the leader of the ragtag group barked, naming the regal Nepentha by a country term that ranked her not much higher than a walker of the streets. Jani gasped and Nepentha's full lips compressed tighter than ever.

"Speak now or die!" The woman's eyes flashed as cold as the metal of the sword she held before her.

"Do you dare accost a daughter of the light?" Nepentha demanded in outrage. "Have you sold your soul to the darkness, then?" she jeered.

"Ay-ee!" The russet-haired leader slashed out with a speed that astonished the granary clerk, but her attack was halted by a soft cry behind her.

"No, Dunkil! By the Light, no!"

A tall, cruelly thin figure advanced, his own russet thatch stiff with gray, his sightless blue eyes clear as he halted with an unerring sense of space by his sister's side. For despite the differences in age and gender, their resemblance was marked. The man bowed his head with a gentle humility.

"Forgive us, fellow-travelers! But those who serve the light are few and far between in these hills."

The whip-thin woman beckoned. Two members of her party stepped forward to take hold of the bridles of Nepentha's and Jani's mounts.

"Come, Dafydd." She touched her brother's arm. "We must clear the pass. It's not safe to linger."

"Please," the blind Dafydd turned his gaunt features to Nepentha. "We too serve the light. We too," he added with composure, "seek to throw off the yoke of the forces of Da'a and to protect the Q'tar!"

Nepentha's indrawn breath sparked a small hard glint of amusement in Dunkil's gaze.

Dunkil's band was camped in a series of caves high above the valley which held Taavel. The lights of the quiet city below glittered like a faint reflection of the stars. The woman Dunkil nodded at the lights below their camp.

"Zaavan's Sindren allies hold all the land from Halfern to Taavel. To the east, Chabal V'na holds sway, while Gagues of Dravan has had to spread his forces nearly to Tabor. It seems that news of the Q'tar has run like wildfire through the Quettar mountain and desert tribes. Gagues has his hands full. Mamut is totally lost to the dark. Not a flicker of resistance is felt there."

"What of Elfarn?" Jani questioned. Quan Matar threw her a quick look of respect.

"Much like Halfern—wherever word of the Q'tar spreads, hope and rebellion take root."

Nepentha interrupted, annoyed at this talk of politics.

"It is imperative that we reach Taavel," she insisted. "Together with one who abides within the city, we can contact the holy city of light. With the power which lies therein, the Q'tar can be found and brought to the light."

Quan Matar stirred at this and cleared his throat.

"The Q'tar must come to the light freely, Nepentha," he reminded her. She brushed his objection aside as of no consequence.

"He cannot choose the dark, granary clerk!" she dismissed his concerns. "And if we cannot ride into Taavel, then this seer must come to us. Jani, Quan Matar," she gestured to her companions with rising impatience, "to me."

"Is this wise?" Dunkil asked as the three from Altari-Maro linked hands, although with reluctance on the part of Jani and Quan Matar.

"Silence! I will not be denied!" The silver-shot threads in Nepentha's dark crown of hair appeared to take light from the stars as the three concentrated upon their linked hands.

Behind the small grouping, starlight coalesced, intensified. Several among Dunkil's company came to their feet, weapons out. Dunkil flung out an arm, too late, to catch at her brother.

"Stop!" she cried, breaking the mental bond of the seekers.

"You dare!" Nepentha cried, but Dafydd paid their cries no heed, advancing as surely to the light as one sighted. He put out his hand to that brilliance. At his touch, it shimmered and cleared. Within, an ageless, ancient figure shone, seated and flanked by two younger companions. Three pairs of eyes as piercing as the light scanned the group huddled in the cave.

"Dafydd, healer," the old woman's strong voice rang in the enclosed space within the rocks," for your deliverance from the hands of Da'a, we give thanks!" Her severe gaze swept on to Nepentha, awestruck into silence for once.

"Daughter of the light, step forth." The strength of that command made Quan Matar flinch. Jani grasped his arm, her nails digging into flesh. Nepentha stepped before that shimmering triad and curtsied with reverence.

"Do you think, Nepentha, that the City of Light is so far removed from the course of events that we would not be aware that the Q'tar is known?" The soft query brought a dark flush to the tailor's eldest daughter. She dropped to her knees and bowed her head. "He has been received in the heart of Abri-Hataro. Already he moves toward his *m'airi.*

"Arise, my daughter, and listen well. Rein in your eagerness and your pride," she added dryly, "and hear me. Those who have given their hearts to the light have rallied against the dark. Hope exists that this unholy alliance between the Mamut Emperor and the dark god can be broken. That he will be driven back to his graceless temple in the Ma'a'mat mountains, away from the affairs of humans.

"Know this: the Q'tar will come in his own time, if it is to be. The common folk of the Five Crowns are prepared, thanks to the work of Dunkil and others like her in a thousand small farms and towns across the provinces." The Lady paused, gripped the arms of her companions and rose with an effort to stand before the group assembled in the cave.

"Seek you instead for one who comes into these mountains in peril of her life, for she must be brought living to the Q'tar in his hour of need."

"But, my Lady," Nepentha protested, "the Q'tar is but a single vessel, what need has he of another?"

"Do you know all, small daughter, that you may question the light?"

"Forgive me, Lady," the kneeling form of Nepentha shuddered, "but it is my ignorance that prompts my concern."

The Lady sank back into her seat and considered the woman before her as the company crept together behind Nepentha, Dunkil, and Dafydd.

"This Q'tar is like none other known in the history of the light, my children! Hear me, we are all servants of the light. And this young woman, this Jennet, may yet find her path crossing that of the Q'tar. Find her!" She waved a hand across her face and there appeared an image of a young blonde woman, dressed to travel, her features grim.

She waved her hand again and the image was gone. "Find her. Keep her safe. The light depends upon your heart and your courage. For all our sakes, may you succeed!"

The diffused glow in which the three figures from Abri-Hataro were framed began to solidify, to shrink. They were gone in an instant. Nepentha shook her head, rose to her feet, and turned to her companions.

"I don't understand." Her brows twisted in her puzzlement. "Why can the light not reach out and secure this girl? This Jennet?"

"Perhaps," Dafydd reminded her, "because she, like the Q'tar must choose her own path to the light."

"Find her," Quan Matar repeated. Jani, squeezing his hand in hers, surprised the glint of a smile in the depths of those dark eyes as she finished for him, "not take her captive, Nepentha!"

"Keep her safe," Dunkil added, as she surveyed her companions, dismissing Nepentha. "If she's coming through these mountains, there are two directions she can take—towards Halfern or towards the coast."

"Dunkil," Nepentha bit back the sharpness in her tone, tried again. "I—we can help you search. We are seekers."

Taking the measure of Nepentha's sincerity, the Tabor rider swept a rapid gaze over the Altari-Maro woman, made up her mind in that instant, and proffered a hard handclasp of promise.

"Together we will find her."

Chapter 14

Crouched in the lee of a fodder-shelter on the edge of a peasant's field, Patar surveyed the fields about them before sitting back in the shelter with a grunt. Utari had parceled out the journey bread and remnants of dried fruit the Aleri had given them. Since their night raid with the Aleri a fortnight ago, they had crossed the rest of the lake lands of Tabor, dodging sporadic Sindren search parties until fording the Halfus river into Halfern. With that move, the Sindren presence had amplified tenfold.

Patar's frown rippled the muscles of his forehead as he voiced his thoughts.

"It seems to me that we draw the dark god's forces to us like a magnet," He stopped in surprise, eyes gleaming. "We found no red stone on Gagues. Perhaps," he mused, "because none was to be found." After a moment's silence, he turned to Jennet. "Perhaps we should look closer to home. Have you such a stone upon yourself, Jennet?"

Her pale face flushed dark red.

"Does such a one as I go bedecked in jewels? You see before you all that I am, all that I have I carry upon my back." Stung, her voice rose in anger. "Shall I seize my pack and spill its contents before you?" Suiting action to words, she dragged her pack from its resting place, halted by Patar's fierce whisper.

"Nay, Jennet! You do wrong me!" he exclaimed. "I would not name you traitor! I meant only, perhaps this Sindren window comes by chance through something of yours."

Jennet hugged her pack to her thin frame, then glanced up at Patar.

"I have seen a red gem. *He*—the Q'tar—wears a deep red garnet set round with wild gold on his left hand."

Utari looked from one to the other of his companions.

"When I lay down my flute, I feel our contact still," he commented.

Patar pursed his lips, nodded once, twice.

"Just so. In your tie to the Q'tar," he began and Jennet finished his thought for him.

"I may have been linked in more subtle ways?" She shook her head. "It seems farfetched, Patar Q'an. But," she raised great blue eyes, bruised with weariness, to him, "how then can I put the past away from me, if your thoughts follow true?"

"There is this, Jennet-child," Patar rested his hand on her shoulder. "We can send you safely back to Abri-Hataro."

Mutinously, the set of her chin and the tension of her body expressed her opposition to his suggestion with soundless eloquence.

"I thought as much," Patar's grin came and went.

"I will leave you both and travel alone," Jennet began, shaking her head as both Patar and Utari rolled their eyes at her suggestion.

"We go on, little one," Patar rejoined and cleared his throat. "Truly your path does not lie in the City of Light, else you would have remained within the safety of Abri-Hataro with our Lady of Light. But, we stick together. So far," his grin twitched, "we haven't done so badly, eh my friends? Which way now? Over the Naransai into Ameridia or farther east into Halfern?"

Jennet was conscious of their gaze upon her, of the tug of her heart like a directional signal. Patar read that lightning flash of desire.

"Halfern it is, my friend."

Seated in the middle of the canoe, Utari kneeling before her and Patar behind, Jennet found herself relaxing for the first time in weeks as they traversed the placid twilight waters of the River Settern. The mild breeze teased them with the merest hint of spring to come. Winter had buffeted the holdings of Halfern—one strong storm after another dropping snow falls frosty and thick that one week later melted in sudden thaws, only to be followed by precipitous low temperatures that left the land ice-coated and frozen once more. Yet this small twining breeze stirred the slightest of ruffles on the surface of the water as they paddled down the river with a silent, smooth motion across shadows and light alike. The breeze brought with it the smell of newly budded forests, restless flocks in the river pastures, and the startled piping of a costawit from its reedy nest.

The Halfern countryside was rolling, quiet and deep-rooted. Those fields and homesteads glimpsed from the river's bed had been carved from wilderness so long ago that almost one had the perception of paddling one's way into the ancient, living past. Half-drowsing, Jennet drank in the peace, the sights and sounds of the old country settling itself for the night, and with a deliberate effort eased her mind of its constant harrying worries. She might have been coming home, slipping in under the edge of darkness to a sturdy gray-stone holding with the fires just lit in the keeping room, a pot bubbling on the hearth, two cats stirring on the wide windowsill, and an old blind nurse serenely rocking a somnolent two-year-old before the fire. The door latch lifted—the corner of her mouth lifted—why not, Jennet thought with a bittersweet longing—why not play out the scene to her own whimsical end? And so, in her mind's eye, she watched as the door latch lifted and a dark-haired man strode into the keeping room, curls unruly from the wind, step still as springy as an eighteen-year-old lad's, his face tempered by laughter and, yes, by love.

Running, now stumbling, Jennet drew in her breath on a ragged sob and pressed her tortured lungs for more air. As if a lodestone had drawn her, the thought beat at her, she had brought them all to disaster as soon as they'd left the river behind and set out on land. Behind her came the baying of the grinder hounds and the crackle of flame as a lieber-saber flashed through the underbrush. Blindly she picked herself up and ran on. Her pursuers and their hunting hounds must follow her, else how could she spare Patar and Utari?

Chapter 15

Two elderly, vacant-staring priests threw handfuls of incense into the black tripod holders on either side of the altar. Gray-green fumes, heavy with an acrid, musky scent, escaped from the decorative grills of the incense holders and rose in turgid spirals about the high priest. Kneeling on the hard stone before the mask of Da'a, Chabal V'na drew the god-pleasing smoke deep into his lungs and released his breath with a slow exhalation. From a case offered by his personal attendant, he selected a thong, and dismissed the others.

Alone before the mask, he lit the red candle that symbolized the god-heart and caressed the supple black thong he'd taken from his case, letting the leather slide through his long fingers. Ranged down the center of the thin strap was a series of rakar fangs—sharp as the bite of the living serpent from which they were taken. Inhaling the cloud of burning incense, Chabal V'na began the Fourth Chant of Purification and with deliberation and rising ecstasy, drew the thong down the length of his tongue.

Thick globules of bright red blood dripped onto the offering stone as the temple leader opened his eyes and put back his hood. His lips moved in the phrases of a supplication prayer known only to the inner circle of the Sindren elite. Before him, the god-mask gleamed in the red flame and took on a faint sheen as of perspiration from the heat and heavy incense. Deep within those wells of darkness that were meant as eyes into this world, life stirred. An awareness gathered, focused a will and a power upon the figure of the priest. Power emanated from the mask of Da'a in tangible waves that radiated like an icy warmth—searing yet not burning the flesh of the man.

At length that sense of life faded until only the eyes of the mask held Chabal V'na. How the old god hungered! Yet, *He* could not pour himself into his loyal vassal—to do so would only kill Chabal V'na and a dead servant was no weapon at all. No, what was needed was the boy—the living vessel—the dark god's means of entry into this world. The black will of Da'a flared at the thought, licking at Chabal V'na's exposed face like the kiss of the rakar serpent. Chabal V'na did not flinch at that touch, but prostrated himself before the mask until his cramped limbs reminded him of that outer world. At last he rose stiff in every muscle, swept his hood high to cover the mark of favor burnt into his flesh, and walked with returning vigor toward the courtyard.

Sweeping her field glasses across the Plain of Esdraegon, Dunkil shifted her lean frame to the right to accommodate Nantis as he slid to ground beside her and took the proffered lenses.

"Humph," was his only comment, his pale gray eyes unreadable as always. The rough homespun of his sleeve brushed her arm as he returned the glasses, bringing a fleeting smile to her face.

Below them on the plain, a Sindren command was spread out across the arid expanse. A column of dust from the northwest had drawn her attention, and, as she and Nantis focused on the encampment, a bustle of activity broke the mid-day stillness about the central tent. The column of soldiers which rode in from the northwest halted at the central tent. Its flaps parted and a Mamut commander strode forth with a complement of Sindren priests at his heels.

As an automatic reflex, Dunkil surveyed the mounted line of riders. Abruptly she checked her survey and returned to a lone figure with a breathless whistle. Passing the field glasses with a nod to Nantis, she was slithering down from their observation aerie before Nantis had trained his sights on the Sindren captive—a young woman, long blonde hair tangling about her shoulders, cloakless and hands bound to the pommel of her saddle.

Jani eyed Nepentha with apprehension as the dark-haired seeker blanched.

"The girl! In the hands of those Sindren curs!" Her chin swept up and her green eyes glittered with a hard determination. "We must go in and retrieve her!"

"I agree."

Nepentha, prepared to argue with the Tabor guerilla leader, was nonplussed when Dunkil concurred without a fight.

"A diversion in the night or small hours of the morning before full light should create enough havoc to allow us to attempt a rescue."

"Yes," Nepentha added, her voice harsh, "before the dark forces can use her to reach the Q'tar."

"Or before she comes to harm," Quan Matar put in from where he sat with Jani listening to the conversation. Nepentha flushed, opened her mouth, and closed it.

"If their mounts could be stampeded into the supply carts, we could achieve several ends at once," Jani offered the suggestion. Dunkil threw her a quick, startled glance.

"Just so."

As quiet as a fox coming to ground, Nantis appeared beside Dunkil.

"They've put the prisoner away from the center in a tent guarded by two priests. There is this, also, one rider came in alone shortly thereafter from the mountains—east of us. He was shown into the command post at once."

"But why," Nepentha wondered, her unease apparent, as they regrouped to plan their rescue attempt, "why would a rider be coming from Altari-Maro?"

"Messages from Chabal V'na?" Dunkil suggested without pleasure. "I don't like it. Hurry—let us rejoin the others and make ready our plan of attack. We might succeed against that rabble," a negligent shrug in the direction of the Esdraegon Plain indicated the forces camped there, "but not if Chabal V'na sends reinforcements."

The night was well-gone when Quan Matar and Jani slipped into position.

"Like sending a wasp against a water buffalo!" Quan Matar mumbled with a low sigh and Jani muffled a nervous giggle.

The Sindren Corps' field leaders, like most of their brethren, suffered from a complacent attitude based on superior weapons and numbers. The infidels, it was pointed out to any with the temerity to ask, struck only against unmanned targets. But this group of Corpsmen, as the rebels had seen, counted a Mamut army man among its commanders. Would he be more cautious? Out here on a plain that had no resources to attract rebel interest? *'Well,'* the granary clerk shrugged to himself, *'we shall soon find out.'*

Dunkil, one of the riders, should even now be slipping like a shadow alongside the Sindren mounts with her chosen cohorts. He and Jani and the others were to make sure the horses stampeded into the camp. Nepentha and Nantis should have reached the far side of the plain's encampment, ready to penetrate the untidy city of tents and free the Sindren prisoner.

"Quan Matar," Jani breathed the words next to him, "prepare yourself. Someone moves among the mounts."

A whiplash struck against the night air and a horse jumped in panic, striking against another mount as it came down. The whip cracked once more. Another horse reared in fright, found itself free of the picket line, and bolted forward in a blind panic. Over and over the whip lashed at the air, sending frightened horses in all directions. Quan Matar and Jani rose up like specters and flapped cloaks in front of the milling horses, turning back a galloping rush in their direction. Cries of consternation could be heard issuing from the camp. The minimal complement of night guards was rousing the rest of the camp as squealing, rearing horses crashed against the two-wheeled supply carts, toppling them and trampling their contents.

Quan Matar grabbed for Jani's hand when a lieber-saber cut a swathe in the air near the former picket lines. "Come on," he hissed, "retreat's in order!"

Jani half-turned, running and stumbling against her companion as several skittish Sindren mounts thundered past them. Quan Matar snatched Jani back against the safety of an overturned supply cart. She stuck her head above its side and ducked as a lieber-saber struck beyond them. The Corpsmen were using the sabers to try and head off the stampede to herd the crazed mounts toward the camp perimeter. *'Definitely time to be gone!'* Quan Matar thought and tugged hard on Jani's arm.

"Quickly!" In his impatience to be gone, he tugged at her arm again as she resisted. All of a sudden she gave way, nearly knocking him over in the process. They sorted themselves out and ran headlong now for cover, heedless of noise. Under cover of the milling, frightened horses and frantic shouts from the camp, who would hear?

The gates of the Sindren complex swung wide and an elite Mamut and Sindren cadre rode forth. Isman-Bati quirked a brow and mouthed a silent comment to Obal.

"Chabal V'na."

In a tearing hurry, Obal noted and sent a fervent prayer to any god that would care to answer that the Sindren priest did not take the coastal road. The last wagon packed, Assir climbed aboard, looked to his father for a signal, and fell in behind as Obal shook the reins for his team to move out. Two covered wagons of finished goods were on their way to market at Halstev. Barak lay propped up in relative comfort behind Assir, well out of sight within the wagon. Mari-Isman stayed behind, dealing with dyers and fleece merchants as capably as her mate.

Their luck held. Obal glanced at Isman and grinned with relief. Chabal V'na's company rode steadily along the western road toward the Naransai. Although his hands itched to set his team at that same brisk pace, Obal restrained himself and gritted his teeth at the decorous pace they would be forced to endure if they hoped to avoid notice.

Nepentha winced, but did not cry out as Nantis' grip tightened about her waist. He half-dragged her up the incline toward the sheltered haven where their ragged troop regrouped.

"By the Light!" he exclaimed.

The tailor's eldest daughter opened her eyes with an effort, letting Nantis guide her to her feet, all her will concentrated on keeping conscious and upright. A dark shadow detached itself from a boulder, and a burly member of their band took shape. He swept the Altari-Maro seeker into his arms, careful to avoid the clumsily bound left arm, and followed as Nantis quickened his pace.

They found their companions short by four—one man had not been seen since the stampede started. Another had taken the brunt of a lieber-saber, deliberately, his partner reported, voice stripped of emotion, to draw attention away from the rest of their saboteurs. The final two—Quan Matar and Jani—had not returned, nor could any account for their absence. Dunkil took one look at Nepentha and called for her brother Dafydd.

"And all for naught? You did not reach the prisoner?" Dunkil lifted a grim face to her fellow hillmen.

"Nay," Nantis contradicted her, "we made our way with some small difficulty to the prisoner's tent. But came too late. She was not found within. Getting out again, this one took a saber along her arm."

"Gone?" Dunkil hissed between her teeth. "But!" Her dark eyes narrowed. "Unless she had other means of fleeing?"

"Then she would not have been a captive, yes?" Nantis suggested as Dafydd hurried forth and knelt at Nepentha's side. The Altari-Maro woman cried out in pain as his fingers eased her makeshift bindings. The healer's long fingers hesitated.

A gentle sigh of sound swept through the darkness of their camp. It swelled, gathered into melody. Nantis and Dunkil turned as one towards the source of that music as four figures stepped into the small clearing. A thin young man, flute raised to his lips, entered first, followed by Quan Matar and Jani, who flanked a broad-shouldered older man. As the flute's notes drifted to quietness, Nepentha stilled beneath Dafydd's skilled touch. In spite of his outer blindness, he deftly cut away the scorched sleeve, cleansing and salving the wound that would render the arm useless for a long time. As he rebandaged it, Dunkil and Nantis took their measure of the newcomers.

Quan Matar indicated the taller man.

"Patar Q'an, Dunkil. From the City of Light!"

Patar inclined his head, touched the flutist.

"Utari. We were companions to the young woman whom you sought to free from Sindren hands." His fierce dark eyes swept the camp. "She remains, then?"

Once more, Nantis explained.

Patar's brows drew together in a frown.

"This I do not understand."

Jani loosened her hold on Quan Matar's hand and cleared her throat. "Before we fell back, Quan Matar and I, from our position, some horses came through. Well," she added, throwing up her hands, "lieber-sabers were glowing everywhere like demon-worms from the Great Dry Swamp. We thought it best to get away. But," she hurried to finish her tale, "I thought... I thought one horse came through from the encampment that carried a rider."

"Are you sure?" Patar and Dunkil asked together.

Jani nodded, her round eyes solemn.

"Fairly certain. One figure, hunched over, bulky. Odd, that. I couldn't make it out."

"Someone," Nantis ventured, "taking advantage of the confusion to slip away unseen from the Sindren camp?"

"The girl?" Dunkil directed her terse query to Patar, who shook his head.

"No. No," he repeated with obvious regret, "Jennet is resourceful, but I have tried to touch her and cannot. She would have come to me if she were free."

"Lendl," Dunkil picked out a slight, older man from their company. "Which way?" she demanded of Jani.

"East."

"Lendl, circle east about the encampment below. Watch for signs of a heavily-laden horse."

A brief flash of white teeth against the night sky marked him as Lendl disappeared into the gloom.

"We'll soon know." Dunkil turned back to Patar, hesitated, and introduced herself, Dafydd, Nantis, and told Patar of their fight, the appearance of the Lady, and their subsequent quest to locate Jennet.

"And now?" Patar asked.

"Now we wait."

Within the hour a swift patter of gravel marked the return of Lendl, who dismounted and gave his horse into eager hands as he made his way to Dunkil and Nantis to report. Patar sat up.

"One horse. A heavy burden—two passengers or one rider and heavy gear?" He suggested the last as a possibility, but it was clear he did not believe it to be so.

"Which way?"

"East."

"Toward Halstav and the Halfern free harbor," Patar stated with conviction.

"Away from Altari-Maro and Chabal V'na," Nantis amended that assessment.

Dunkil clapped the tired Lendl on the shoulder.

"Good work, Lendl. Take your rations and rest while we break camp. By daybreak we needs must be further along the foothills if we hope to bypass that vermin-ridden horde camped on the plain below. We ride for Halstav and this woman."

"But who," Jani pondered in an aside to those resting by Nepentha's side, "who is't can be named friend within that nest of rakar-snakes that would have freed the prisoner?"

Patar's voice came out of the darkness.

"Perhaps was no friend, Jani. Perhaps it was one who seeks Jennet for his own purposes?"

Zaavan twisted the cape from his prisoner's head, with a roughness that displayed his rising frustration that the girl had not been moved to trust him. For three days now they had been riding like a wind-dragon for Halstav and escape. He had known, when Chabal V'na's personal dog arrived in camp to see Jaken, the Mamut commander, that Chabal V'na had decided to join the hunt for the girl and the Q'tar himself. What a stroke of good fortune that the Sindren troops had managed at last to run her to ground! Yes, it was his *m'airi* at work—he was destined to have the boy in his hands and his alone. If he'd ever had any doubts, those were put to rest now when the girl was brought into camp right before his eyes. And before he could plan how to take her, another stroke of good fortune—the rebels had chosen this night to steal horses from the Sindren encampment. In all the confusion, there would be no doubt that the girl had escaped to the rebels.

Running now ahead of the Emperor's dogs, Zaavan commandeered fresh mounts for himself and his prisoner—so that pursuit, if it came—and surely it would sooner or later when the dogs got wind of her passage—was left far behind. Old Jaken could be discounted; he was stupid enough to believe his prisoner had escaped with the rebels. Zaavan thought of the bloodstained cloak with his emblem which he'd artfully dropped amidst the cut reins of the Sindren horses. Even now the Mamut commander would be scouring the Naransai foothills, hoping to retrieve his lost prisoner before Chabal V'na could arrive. The cloak was good enough to fool Jaken, but never Chabal V'na! That one, however, would come too late to the Plain of Esdraegon to make any difference at all!

Thus reassured by his thoughts, Zaavan pushed the unresisting girl ahead of him into the Emperor's way-station.

"On the orders of Chabal V'na," he snapped at the startled attendant. "Fresh mounts for me and my prisoner—as well as food and drink. Quickly!" he snarled as the hulking priest shuffled away.

The girl sat with eyes downcast, eating what was put before her without a murmur. As slow-witted as any village slut, Zaavan decided with distaste. How could such as she have eluded the Sindren Corps' finest in all these past months? Once he was beyond the reach of the High Priest, he would force her to tell him where the boy cowered in hiding. He would have no further use for this drab, frightened creature then.

Jennet might have felt that cold wave of animosity, for she shivered and avoided catching her captor's eyes. Despite his false assurances to the contrary, she harbored no doubts about this man's intentions. So be it. When the time came and he demanded that which she could not give—knowledge of Aedan's whereabouts, she would pretend otherwise and delay and lead him as far astray as possible before he saw through her ruse and killed her. And that was an anguished, bitter thought. She wanted fiercely to live—to see Aedan once again, but if it was not to be, at least she would die secure in the knowledge that she had not delivered him into the hands of the dark god's forces!

"You there," Zaavan accosted their server as the man passed by their table carrying a heavy tray of dirty dishes, "how far to the next village?"

"Not far—a half day's ride come morning, sir." The man's untidy shock of nut-brown hair bobbed as he raised his chin with a glimmer of pride, "and no village, either. She be a fair-sized town, is Harsfeld. A proper inn for travelers, too."

"More ale," Zaavan dismissed the man without a word of thanks or a copper penny for his help. Harsfeld, eh? He recalled the road to Halstav. A half day to Harsfeld. Another half day's ride to the Halfern port. One day and he would have the boy within his grasp. His dark lips curved into the semblance of a smile, and he drank with relish when his tankard was refilled.

Barak welcomed the sun on his face with a broad, contented sigh. Obal grinned beside him.

"We'll be in Harsfeld by noon today, my friend, then we'll get a decent meal into your stomach!"

"Shh!" Barak tilted a crooked smile at Obal. "Isman is not a bad cook, not bad. We've eaten worse, if I recall. Remember that bitter glop of vainwen seed and ilsop weed they bake into cakes in the backwoods of Elfarn?"

"Ho!" Obal wrinkled his nose with distaste. "Enough said, Barak! Your words alone are near enough to twist my poor stomach into knots! That slimy weed! Those stenchful seeds! I repent! Isman is the finest cook this side of Altari-Maro!"

"I hear thy slanderous tongue, Obal once-friend!" Isman wagged his head in mock-reproof as he and Assir came alongside the first wagon. "Assir frets for his mare. We shall stop at the next likely stream and rest a moment, eh, while he adjusts her harness.

"And for thou, Obal," Isman's broad features winked at his Halfern friends, "I have been saving a basket of Mari's lentil flatbreads."

Obal's brows rose in delighted surprise.

"Methinks I hear the babbling of a sweet little brook just beyond this sunny slope, old friend!"

As the wagons crested the next rise, the sounds of the winding, narrow stream, underfit for its bed, came faintly, drowned out by a man's imperious voice shouting in anger. Assir grinned at Obal and Barak.

"Sweet water, thy Halfern giant? Sounds more like the ravings of a sable-crested river swooper, if my ears do not malign that shad-eater!"

Obal's face darkened and he hauled hard on the reins of the horses pulling his wagon. Handing the lines to Barak with an alacrity that belied his massive frame, he reached within the wagon and pulled out two cloaks. As he drew one cloak about himself, his hand went to the Dravanian dagger he wore at his belt. Barak held on white-faced to the reins of a team made uneasy by the commotion at stream-side.

The sound barely registered as another party of riders approached far back on the road behind them, one lone rider coming fast before the others. Isman heard the riders, glanced back at once and saw no soldiers, only a small party of wayfarers, before his attention was diverted by the sight of Barak huddled over the reins in a muffling cloak, halting his wagon by the side of the road. Obal was nowhere to be seen.

Puzzled, Isman motioned to his son to draw their wagon onto the grassy verge at the edge of the stream at some distance from the taciturn man in rich, plain clothing who was berating his horse with both curses and his crop as it backed away from the onslaught, limping as it did so on its left hind leg. Even as the man turned, a crimson star dangling from one earlobe, he did not lose his hold on the short-reined grip he held on a second mount. Its rider, Isman noted, was a young woman, her features hooded and her hands bound to the pommel of her saddle. Isman stepped down from his wagon as the stranger threw a baleful glance at their party.

"Do not approach!" The man's voice raked Assir as the cloth merchant and weaver's son jumped down and took a tentative step toward the frightened horse. "I am on the Emperor's business! Stand clear!"

Isman fought to keep his eyes averted from the sight of Obal shifting as his bulk like a mountain cat from tree to shrub to boulder as he worked his stealthy way toward the enraged stranger. Barak sat motionless, head bowed beneath the hooded cloak.

"Zaavan!"

At the bellow from Obal, the man spun about. His lips curled in a sneer as he took in the figure of the big Halfern man.

"Would you end your days on a Sindren spit, Halfern offal?" he snarled. "Put away your weapon and flee while you may!"

In response to that taunt, Obal circled nearer, backing Zaavan closer to the horse he fought to control. Within his hooded eyes, a flicker of fear and desperation shone as Obal advanced with slow deliberation.

"You will all be punished if this creature is not stopped!" Zaavan barked in the direction of the wagons. Barak lifted his head and let the hood fall. Zaavan's eyes narrowed.

"So, one cur still runs with the other? And the boy?" The sun flashed as a dagger slid from his sleeve into his hand. Zaavan nicked the leg of his prisoner. "Come closer, Halfern scum, and this woman dies!"

"I do not fear death!" Jennet cried out, her hood falling back as she kneed her horse with an unexpected spurt of energy for one who had sat as stone. Her startled mount jerked forward, dragging Zaavan about as Obal lunged, missing his quarry by the width of his stroke. Regaining his hold on Jennet's horse, Zaavan maneuvered the horse's bulk between himself and Obal. Only the big man's heavy breathing and the strained inhalations of Zaavan broke the sunny morning calm.

Zaavan feinted to his right, slashing out at Obal. Side-stepping the onslaught, Obal ripped the cloth of Zaavan's sleeve as they passed. Pass, feint, parry. Circle around and around the horse's body. Beads of sweat coursed from Zaavan's dark brow. Obal breathing was deep and easy, his eyes never straying from his target's swaying body or his knife hand. Once more Zaavan slashed out before feinting to his left. The sound of gravel spitting beneath a horse's galloping hooves and a wind-fed hail reached the clearing.

"Obal! Barak!"

In that split-second of lost concentration as the big man checked, Zaavan struck, his blade glittering as it arced downward toward Obal's chest. Like the derval bull he so resembled, the Halfern giant swung his massive frame sideways and lunged with his free hand for Zaavan's blade arm. Like a sledge striking fragile tonchil wood, his hand wrapped about that wrist and wrenched his enemy to him in a bone-crushing hug. Zaavan's eyes bulged and his face lost all color.

Caskar catapulted from his horse into the clearing, oblivious to the drama playing out before him.

"Obal! Barak! Chabal V'na comes!"

Barak leaped from his wagon seat, throwing the reins to Assir.

"Obal!"

The glazed expression of Obal's eyes dimmed and he stared at Barak, and then down at the man still struggling beneath the force of his arm. He gave the Sindren follower a final shake like a bear with a tchitchi fish, before flinging him away into a heap in the dirt. Obal moved toward his party, conscious now of Caskar panting hard at Barak's side.

"Obal! Look out!" The shout was torn from Caskar's heaving chest. Even as Obal half-twisted around, light flashed from a blade that marked where his broad back had been a moment before, and then a soft grunt sounded behind him. Recovering his balance, Obal straightened to see the haft of a stout Halfern knife protruding from Za-avan's chest. The knife had marked his heart true and his eyes, opened to the blue sky, no longer saw. Barak stood motionless, his eyes alight with a grim satisfaction.

When he spoke, his voice carried only to Obal's ears.

"A friend's life spared and a death avenged."

A long look passed between the two men. Obal straightened and turned about to the rest of the company, clapping a hand on Barak's shoulder.

"You were a trifle slower than usual, little friend," Obal noted. His grin slid from his face as he moved with surprising swiftness to catch at the bindings of Zaavan's prisoner, where Assir had cut her free. Obal's hand reached for her throat as he cried out.

"Now, this one shall pay for her meddling that cost us Aedan and you a Sindren cell, Barak!"

"No!"

A shrill chorus of voices echoed behind them. So intent had they been on the drama contained in the clearing, that no one had marked the approach of the other party of riders coming along behind Caskar. Confused cries of recognition rang out.

"Dunkil!"

"Isman-Bati!"

"Caskar!"

"Jani?"

Yet, no one moved for fear of precipitating the coldly intent Obal to action, least of all the woman herself until Obal's hand touched her.

She stirred as if to life and cried out.

"Thou dost wrong me, friend-Obal!"

Obal froze. Behind him the babble of voices rose as everyone spoke at once, urging Obal to back away. Then one hoarse voice screeched above the noisy tumult.

"By the Light! Look!"

Quan Matar sat his donkey ramrod stiff, arm thrust to the sky. A collective gasp resounded throughout the clearing as all eyes were riveted upon a glowing stream of pure white light that sang through the clear morning sky and hovered above Obal and Jennet. They watched in awe as the light took on mass and descended. Great white wings seemed to flap at the sky while a head reared back against the sun. The white heart of the dragon Eslevan beat in the full light of day as its form touched earth in front of the stilled tableau. Two molten black eyes appeared to survey the silent onlookers, and then the shimmering stare fixed on Jennet.

Swinging down from her horse as Obal dropped his hold, a bemused smile lit up her pale face. With eager arms she reached out to the form of the dragon.

"Aedan-love!"

Chapter 16

Eslevan's light shifted, coalesced, and Aedan stepped from the heart of the dragon, the brightness of the light shining so about him that it hurt the eyes to look upon him. As the light dimmed away, he clasped Jennet to him in a fervent embrace. Their arms tightened about one another and their lips met in a kiss that seemed to spark the air like a prism shooting back the sun. As the pair turned to the clearing, Obal and Barak reached Aedan at the same moment, hugging him and reproaching him with equal vigor to the astonished dismay of Nepentha.

"You young scamp!" began Barak and Obal finished, cuffing their former charge's shoulder lightly, "would you leave us without word? That your good father were here!"

"Hold! Hold!" Aedan put them both from him and drew Jennet to his side. Patar, Dunkil, and Caskar approached. Nepentha, as pale as Jennet had been earlier, murmured to no one in particular.

"Never have I seen anyone ride the light so!"

"Patar-friend, well met!" Aedan greeted the Lady's trusted aide with a rueful grin. "What purpose is there in this gathering, and," the pleasure in his fine eyes clouded as he took in the crumpled form of his father's former steward, "what further trouble does Zaavan's presence presage?"

"I think, Aedan Q'tar," Patar responded with a bruising clasp of the young man's shoulder, "that Dunkil—our commander here—and young Caskar can best tell our tale."

"Chabal V'na comes," Caskar repeated, jerking a thumb in the direction from which he'd come. "Even now, he and Jaken have joined forces to pursue that one—" he stabbed a finger in the direction of Zaavan's body, "and his hostage." The Halfern lad blushed as he observed Jennet and Aedan's clasped hands.

Aedan's gaze swept the wagons of Isman-Bati, the eager, excited faces of Assir and Utari, the bedraggled band grouped about Nantis, and the seekers clustered by Isman-Bati.

"We came," Dunkil took up the tale, "because this little one," she threw Caskar a quick, affectionate glance, "told us that the Q'tar was known. We have been fighting the length and breadth of the Naransai ever since, nipping at the heels of Chabal V'na's forces. We met these three seekers from Altari-Maro, and through them, the Lady herself from the City of Light commanded us to find and safeguard the lass beside you."

"'Tis so," Patar rejoined. "Jennet and I, along with Utari and his flute's light-song, have been playing the same game from Dravan across Tabor and into Halfern. Yet, we were marked from the beginning in some fashion. The Sindren hounds were ever at our heels and at last took

Jennet as we fled. Utari and I rode with Dunkil to one purpose."

"And you, Barak?" Aedan looked to his old teacher.

"We sought the aid of those same seekers in Altari-Maro when you disappeared from our midst in Taavel."

"Our stay there was prolonged by Barak's usage of a Sindren cell," Obal shot a look of bewilderment at Jennet, but Barak placed a hand on his companion's arm.

"And survived, as all can plainly see. We were on our way to Halstav with Isman and his son Assir, pursuing not this young lady but a further clue to your whereabouts."

"Behind all, then, comes Chabal V'na—drawn by Zaavan," Aedan summed up their position.

"His purpose," Jennet spoke for the first time, "was to use me to reach you, Aedan. Chabal V'na's goal is the same—to take you for the dark god!"

"How far," Aedan addressed Caskar, "are Chabal V'na and his forces behind us?"

"Two days ride along this road."

"Then," Aedan's quick gaze swept the clearing again, "if you will help me consign the husk that was Zaavan to the Light, we will make our way to Halstav. Friends await there who may be of help."

It was a matter of a few minutes only to gather enough dry wood to create a pyre for the crumpled body of Zaavan. One of Dunkil's band laid his body atop the wood, as Aedan, Barak , and Obal stood to one side. Patar, across from them, nodded as his eyes met Aedan's. Focusing upon the wood piled before him, Patar drew a breath in and when he released it with a hiss, smoke curled from the dry wood. In a few minutes, the wood was blazing and Zaavan's form was completely engulfed. Obal turned away without a word and strode off to join Isman-Bati.

When they headed out of the clearing, Jennet rode in Obal's wagon, sequestered in the rear with Aedan. No need to draw attention to themselves with dragons riding the skies, Aedan told them. Dunkil and her riders broke up into twos and threes to drift unnoticed through Harsfeld and on to Halstav. Patar and Utari paced their mounts alongside Isman's wagons. Behind them, smoke drifted skyward as flames consumed Zaavan's body.

Warmth met and mingled, like the banked coals of a fire that now and then sent errant sparks into the air. Content to hold one another in that moving interplay of light and love, at long last Jennet stirred and stole a shy glance at Aedan. So still he sat that he might have slept if she hadn't felt that sense of joy and contentment mingling with her own heightened awareness. His eyes opened at her glance and she jumped as if a rocket had burst within her, showering her with fireworks.

"It was *you*!" she breathed, half in wonderment, half-accusing. "All this time! Warming me, with me!" Her voice faltered.

"Loving you," Aedan countered, his dark eyes serious. "You never guessed?" he asked, and at her mute nod of denial, went on. "As you loved me once when I was unaware. No wonder that you hated me so!"

"No!" Again that quick denial, and then, biting her lip, she met his gaze. "Yes. That was my pride, Aedan. When we were tied, I fought because I thought your love grew only from that forced joining."

His hands caught at her own.

"Leaving you in Abri-Hataro—I almost came back, but...." Now his strong voice hesitated.

"Your path lay elsewhere," Jennet finished for him. "And I saw too late, my love, that my path lay with you—our lives forever intertwined, enmeshed by love."

"Not one life submerged in the shadow of the other," Aedan's lips murmured against the pale blonde fall of hair above her ear.

She twisted about to search his face.

"Exactly. Whatever your *m'airi*, mine comes as companion."

"Nay, Jennet," he shook his head, contradicting her, "your *m'airi* makes my own life—and whatever I accomplish—possible!"

Laughter sparked her blue eyes in the faint light of the enclosed wagon.

"Let us not argue, Aedan-love! I will stop thy false protestations!"

And so she did, and very satisfactorily, Aedan thought as they lapsed into silence, rocked in the secure and comforting confines of the wagon, away from time and all the day's concerns for the remainder of their trip into Halstav.

The port of Halstav sprawled about the narrow harbor that marked the confluence of the mighty Halfern River with Barijt Sound. The deep, fjord-ridden sound lay between the Western continent and the Barrens, a small continent in its own right, but one aptly named. Its western coast was marked by a knife-edged series of fjords that sliced the broad, nearly impenetrable coastal mountain chain that stretched tip to tip from north to south. Beyond the mountains lay a barren desert interior inhabited by an unknown number of small foraging bands, most of whom divided the year between spring and fall camps along the mountain fringes and winter and summer encampments strung along the eastern coast. Far to the south, a single bleak fort represented the easternmost outpost of the Mamut Empire.

The Inn of the One-Eyed Cat sat behind a thorny rose hedge that grew high and thick enough to afford its guests plenty of privacy and peace within. The half-timbered and stone two-story inn offered private staircases and vine-covered balconies at both ends as well. A discreet staff gave attentive, yet unobtrusive service for a fair price, and Isman was well known to the proprietors.

Washed and refreshed, Aedan threw open the door onto his balcony and saw Jennet before him. A tiny undercurrent of excitement ran between them. From within, a knock sounded at the connecting door to the adjacent room. Aedan rolled his eyes; Jennet laughed and took his hand as the door opened and Patar ushered in a servant laden with a heavy tray.

"Eat first, my friends. Dunkil and the others will join us then, yes?"

"Yes," Aedan agreed. "I've made contact with my friends. They will be with us shortly."

As the servant set out their meal, a second knock sounded at the hall door. Barak entered at Aedan's hail and stood before his young friend. Aedan, seeing the paleness of his features and the set of his chin, pulled out a chair from the table which held the tray of food.

"Sit, Barak, sit. Now, what troubles you, old friend?"

Barak opened his palm before Aedan. The dark red gemstone set in a delicate gold ring which lay revealed in Barak's hand absorbed the light and shone with a fiery inner blaze. Aedan's eyes opened wider with astonishment.

"Where?"

"I took this from Zaavan's body before he burned."

With a hand that trembled, Aedan picked up the ring, his forehead wrinkled in bafflement.

"Not mine." He threw Barak a sharp glance, "but like enough to be its twin."

"Yes," Barak admitted, shifting in his chair. "It was the mate to your father's ring, worn by your mother until she put it in the hands of your old nurse, Babil, for safekeeping."

A spasm of remembered pain crossed Aedan's face, and then eased as Jennet's hand sought his in a reassuring grip.

"My mother knew that she would not return to the holding."

Patar cleared his throat.

"We questioned a Sindren captive, Aedan-friend. He told us that his Sindren leader looked to such a stone as this to follow us. We found no stone upon him, however, and none of us wore such."

Aedan touched Jennet's arm.

"Your backpack, Jennet. If you would bring it here to me, please."

Puzzled, she slipped away without protest and returned with her travel-worn pack, which she gave into Aedan's hands. Deep within its folds his fingers probed and at last fetched into view a battered, small leather pouch. Upending it before them, a man's ring of wild gold and garnet dropped beside its delicate, feminine counterpart in Barak's palm. Flushing, Aedan met Jennet's incredulous stare.

"The ring seemed too ostentatious for the City of Light. I took it off. Before I left, I thought perhaps you might accept a farewell token from a friend. When I could not find you, Jennet-love, I met with one of the children—Topay."

Jennet grimaced, the pain of her remembered selfishness still sharp enough to flick its knife-edge against her conscience.

"I never saw it—or Topay. But she's a lively child, full of surprises. She must have hidden the treasure in my pack for me to find later." Her guilt-stricken blue eyes sought Patar's.

"Nay, Jennet-sweet! Now 'tis clear. Zaavan used this stone to seek its mate and found you instead of the Q'tar.

Imagine his frustration as we led him on a wild goose chase, never coming near to the Q'tar!" He laid a hand on Aedan's too-still shoulder. "Think not of blame, young Aedan. With Jennet's taking came we all into the hands of this good company. 'Twas meant, by the Light!"

"Let us be thankful," Barak observed, "while we may. Eat, one and all. We'll be glad of such in the hours which lie before us!"

When the servants had gone again, Dunkil and Nepentha arrived via the courtyard stair. Utari trailed Quan Matar and a rosy-cheeked Jani, whose dark ringlets curled damply on her nape. Settling himself in a corner, Utari took out his constant companion and became absorbed in polishing his flute.

Obal and Isman-Bati strode in from the hall, the Halfern man guiding Assir before him and teasing Isman's oldest son about the pretty hall serving maid. When they had settled themselves within the room, Barak addressed Aedan.

"Your tale hangs upon our ears, Aedan Q'tar. Tell all, from the moment you disappeared in Taavel."

Aedan shifted in his seat, gathered his thoughts, and directed a rueful smile at Jennet, who sat curled up in the chair next to him.

"I was saved from certain death in Taavel by Jennet, who pulled me to safety by the Light's grace. I had known her in my fevered state and thought her but a dream. Together we traveled into the Naransai, searching for the place my mother sought." His dark eyes brooded for a moment on the revelations of that high stone hut, but then he shook his head and returned his attention to the gathering before him.

"The Light, it seems, found us. We were transported to Abri-Hataro—the City of Light." Aedan looked around the group. "My place was in this world. I left that shining city and its graceful inhabitants to search out my friends and to fight the grip of Empire and Corps—to regain at least my father's holding from the dark god's hand."

"But now!" Nepentha forgot herself, rose, and towered over them, her eyes shining. "Thou art the Q'tar! With such a one as thee, the Lady and all of the Light may focus their power against the dark and drive it from the Western lands!"

Barak glowered at the tailor's daughter. Obal nudged his friend while Isman-Bati's thoughtful gaze rested on Jennet.

"If it be his will," the weaver dropped his gentle reminder into the hush which followed Nepentha's impassioned remarks. She rounded on him, but subsided with difficulty as Isman encouraged Aedan. "Thy tale is not yet ended, is this not so?"

A sudden clatter sounded on the stairs. Caskar burst into the room.

"Nantis reports the approach of Chabal V'na and his troops—no more than a few hours ride from Halstav!"

Voices clamored for attention. Barak gesticulated before Nepentha, while Obal placed his bulk between his former charge and the tumult erupting around him. Jennet reached Patar as Dunkil questioned Caskar. Only Isman-Bati remained seated, one brow rising in a mild query at Aedan's unperturbed demeanor.

Aedan closed his eyes.

Isman blinked. So!

Aedan opened his eyes as two figures appeared beside him. Startled, Dunkil drew her sword as the hubbub subsided in a collective gasp. Two women flanked the Q'tar. The Lady stood on his right, her gray robe emphasizing her height and her majesty. A younger, vivid, dark-haired woman appeared on his left in a brilliant red robe worn over black leather breeches tucked into supple black boots.

"The Lady, you know," Aedan reminded his companions. He indicated the younger woman. "Aleisha—daughter of dragons—heir to the Dogon of the Eastern Empire!"

"Tell me, how I may help you, little dragon-brother?" Aleisha's honeyed tones seemed to reach into the very soul of those gathered before the Q'tar.

Aedan indicated the Lady.

"My allegiance and my honor I lay before thee, Lady of the Light. My dragon-kin stands beside me, as thou can see."

The Lady's shrewd, clear gaze took in Aleisha with approval.

"I have seen thy light, Aleisha, and have known thee by other names in other times and travels. Welcome, Yltras the Red!"

The Lady turned, her glance raking the crowded, tense room. "Jennet." Her hand came out and Jennet slipped from Patar's side to kneel before the ancient figure.

"Nay, rise." As Jennet rose, the Lady looked at Aedan's somber face. "The two of you were once soul-tied. That tie was not forged by some village Elder's wish, but by a deeper power, by the Light itself.

"Together, you may do more than bear the weight of the Light's power against the Sindren Corps. Together," her strong voice surged with hope, not an eye blinked as she surveyed those ranged before her, "together," she repeated, "we may send Da'a back to the hole from which he was birthed! Wilt thou accept the challenge, Q'tar, knowing that death may await thee if we fail?"

His hand somehow linked with Jennet's, Aedan stepped forward. Two voices joined, resounded in the nerve-tautened silence.

"We shall not fail!"

Obal's arms went around Aedan with a mighty roar. He was lifted above the crowd that echoed Obal's hurrah. Behind them, Aleisha met the Lady's troubled glance with a calm smile.

The company parted to prepare themselves. Stepping onto the outside stair a short time later, Jennet saw Obal below her in the courtyard, fussing with his horse. On an impulse, she descended the stairs and crossed the yard to the big Halfern man.

He flushed and shifted his weight as he caught sight of Jennet approaching.

"Please," she entreated him, candid blue eyes meeting his own.

"I thought you were aligned with those priestly carrion-eaters," Obal answered. "I swore to kill you when Barak was taken and Aedan was lost to us."

Jennet ducked under the horse's neck and faced Obal with a hint of a rueful smile flitting across her features.

"I put myself from his side by my own stubborn pride," she admitted, still cross with herself, "yet I could not banish him from my thoughts. By the Light, I saw you and your friends that night. When we all, it seems, sought Aedan's whereabouts. I saw, too, the Sindren forces sweeping towards your fellow seekers. I tried to warn you." Her voice faltered. "I'm sorry Barak was captured."

Obal shrugged.

"'Tis I who am sorry, Jennet. My thoughts flee before my anger and that is all too ready to flare. Mayhaps the two of us can bury the past now and look to the present?"

Jennet's smile widened, and she took the hand he offered.

"And to the future, friend-Obal, should all come right this day!"

They rode out of Halstav at Aedan's insistence. No need, he told them, for an entire city to be drawn into battle. He would have gone on the Light, had he known all too well that Barak and Obal would have refused to be left behind. After nearly an hour's ride, the dust of Chabal V'na's army could be seen in the distance.

A sudden wild gust of wind shrieked past them with such force it tore one's breath away. The Lady halted her companions with an upraised hand. Patar helped her to dismount. She faced her small band of followers; her eyes measured Caskar's face as he tried in vain to still the trembling of his lips.

"Will you hold my mount?"

Caskar slipped from his spotted kerser stallion and bobbed his head, leading the Lady's restive mare away with a reassuring pat. Aedan dismounted, handing the reins of his horse to Nantis as Jennet turned a curious stare on Aleisha, who was helping Patar steady the Lady. The wind had gone, leaving an odd, mind-numbing chill behind. The dark god, the god borne in the high, cold mountains off Mamut—who chilled the heart and drained it of life, made his presence known. Aedan looked to the north and thought of the holding. How simple a life for a simple man! He was a son of the holding, not some earthly kin to dragon-legends! How easy to wish himself elsewhere, anywhere but here in this futile, last-ditch effort to stop the weight of the Empire and the Sindren Corps from crushing the life from the Western world!

Trembling in the cold, Aedan felt a warm hand close about his own and saw Jennet's steadying glance surveying the horizon where the heavy dust clouds thrown up in Chabal V'na's haste rolled closer and closer to their position. His *m'airi*, he understood, sent the shiver up his spine. The choice was made, freely given to the Lady and the Light. He would not run away.

A strange tingling seized him as his heart beat faster. As when he'd drunk the dragon-wine, he felt lightheaded, empty. Standing before him, the Lady intoned a chant that lit the dust-embellished gloom about them with a dancing flicker of golden light. It brightened the day with a hazy sheen. Patar's voice joined her, followed by Nepentha and Quan Matar, Jani and Isman-Bati. Dunkil and Nantis flanked Obal and Barak, who stood grim and steadfast and perspiring in spite of the cold, on either side of Aedan and Jennet. Utari held his flute and waited astride his mount, positioned behind Caskar.

As the haze cleared, Jani's voice faltered for a moment. In a line before them, lathered from days of hard riding, the Emperor's troops fanned out the length and breadth of the horizon. A lone black charger detached itself from the army and galloped forward, stopping shy of the small contingent of the Light.

The Lady lifted her hand in a quick, forbidding gesture.

"Thou who waits behind the husk of thy servant, Chabal V'na, be gone! Back to thy mountainous lair, back to the darkness! Be gone from this world!"

Chabal V'na threw back his head and laughed—a harsh, grating chuckle that seemed to well up out of a bottomless pit. His hood slipped to his shoulders. Sickened, Jani turned her dark eyes away in revulsion at the sight of the deeply entrenched, puckered scars that seamed the features of the Sindren priest into an angry red morass of dead tissue. Chabal V'na flicked his fingers in the direction of the small group before him. Caskar fell to his knees, choking and gasping, frightened horses neighing behind him.

At once, a high bright note of light was loosed into the day as Utari's agile fingers and lips caressed his flute. Caskar's gasps subsided and he struggled to his feet to lean against his nervous, blowing stallion.

Chabal V'na's eyes began to glow until they filled with a blazing red haze. The cold that permeated the day plucked at warmth and light alike until a gray, chill miasma seeped into their very marrow and set Nepentha's teeth to chattering. Aedan could feel Jennet's hand trembling in his own numb grasp.

The Lady retreated back a step, her hands stretching out to meet those of Aleisha and Patar.

"From the foul depths of evil were thou spawned, Da'a!" Aleisha's voice rang out. Flute spiraled and Aleisha sang,

"Comes Yltras and Eslevan! This one
Who is like a brother to dragons
Soars with the light-song, his fire-heart
Wielding the sun like a sword! Banish
The darkness from day! This is the final
Observation of the Quoran Dru!"

Aleisha's song burnt away the mind-numbing paralysis that had settled over Aedan. Light seemed to fill him. He could feel it rushing through him as though he were a living lieber-saber. This, then, was what it meant to be the Q'tar! He did not fight that flow, but welcomed it and felt within himself the presence of some other force—some flood of cold that sought to channel itself through him, to force that stream of light back against its wielders!

Da'a! The dark god! Da'a could use the empty vessel that was the Q'tar even as those of the light did. Anger rose in Aedan. Da'a would not use him to reach those defenders of the light! He was a dragon-son! Rage flamed within him, battering at the cold touch of Da'a. The flames surged and beat at that frozen, unclean power. It did not advance, but neither did it retreat. Frustration deepened his rage; Aedan felt he must be consumed by the battle waging within him.

At that moment, a small insistent note rang in his head and his eyes opened to meet the far-sighted gaze of Jennet. Her blue eyes gleamed with a fire of their own. Her grip tightened on his hand. Together! The light that fed the sword within, the spirit of the dragon—all useless without guidance! With that realization, he held to Jennet's presence and felt her hand in his as together they reached for the lieber-saber that was the Light and aimed it into the very center of that stream of darkness and cold that threatened to overwhelm them all.

The light-song directed their effort and through their small company more light poured in from Abri-Hataro and Altari-Maro, fed and strengthened by all the scattered souls who fought the dark god and his Sindren blight. Down, down into that chill morass that was the heart of Da'a they plunged. The light fluttered on the wings of the red dragon mother and in the spirit of Eslevan. Aedan felt the first spasm of fear in the dark god as Da'a took a step in retreat, and then another and another. Back one step after another he fled the light, withdrawing toward the safety of his Ma'a'mat stronghold. The Light pursued. Quicker now, before Da'a could reach that mountain fastness! Aedan drew upon reserves of strength he hadn't known he possessed, felt Jennet's power expanding, and together they thrust the lieber-saber into the ragged heart of the cold.

In that instant, light arced and flared, throwing them backward in a blinding wash of vermilion and orange and yellow flames. Aedan could not tell if still he held to Jennet. A swelling roll of sound roared out of the bowels of the mountains, engulfing all consciousness.

The acrid stench of burning flesh brought Aedan retching to his knees. Struggling to get up, he forced gritty lids to open and gagged again at the sight which befell his blurred vision. Barak and Obal supported him, while next to him, Aleisha and Patar Q'an clustered about the Lady. She held Jennet's head in her lap. Even as his anxious sight cleared, those blue eyes fluttered open and met his with welcome recognition before they closed in utter exhaustion.

Beyond their huddled group, a blackened drift of smoke marked the remnants of Chabal V'na and his charger. The army behind lay scattered and broken, like stick figures flung before a tornado. Dazed individuals dragged themselves and companions away in all directions.

With the Lady's touch upon him and a cup of dragon-wine to restore him, Aedan slept the night away in his room at the Inn of the One-Eyed Cat. By mid-morning of the next day, he was eager to leave his bed in search of Jennet, when Barak shushed his irritated protestations with a finger. Over the bustle of the hall, Jennet's forceful voice was raised in like furor. Grinning, Aedan allowed Barak to help him dress.

In the light, airy dining room of the inn, Aedan linked his fingers with Jennet's and faced his friends. His dark eyes, still troubled, sought the serene gaze of the Lady, Aleisha glowing beside her.

"My Lady," he entreated, his voice hoarse with foreboding, "I fear we have failed thee."

Outraged, Nepentha's and Obal's loud cries erupted in unison. "You have defeated Da'a! The Q'tar lives!"

"But what of Da'a?" Aedan addressed the Lady. "Pushed once more into his temple stronghold until he regains power enough to win free once more? A poor victory at best."

"Nay, little brother!" A twinkle sparkled in the depths of Aleisha's smile, a smile shared by the Lady and Patar, whose deep eyes held a peace that Jennet could not ever remember having glimpsed there before. Then it came to her—Aisha, his lost wife, had come to peace as well. The Lady nodded her approval and Aleisha continued. "Thy dragon-heart flowered within thee, Aedan-brother. With thy soul's partner didst thou serve as no Q'tar has ever served before.

"Thou didst shape the Light into a mighty sword that bit deep into the dark god. Truly, if he did not die, he may never recover from his wounding to face the wrath of the Light again!"

Aedan's gaze flickered to Jennet, whose earnest features sought confirmation of Aleisha's words from her lady. The strain that lingered and cast a shadow about her face lifted and a sigh escaped her as the Lady addressed them.

"'Tis true. Thou didst more than chase him to his dungeon-temple. But whether he lives or not, Aedan—Jennet and thou—between thou two—have shown us that the Light has much to learn—of dragons and of love! Now rest, children. Thy world awaits thee, the Sindren scourge is broken, and Mamut's empire will soon end at its borders."

Chapter 17

Lailiki blossoms wafted in a fragrant, blushing cloud down upon the tranquil, undulating surface of the River Settern. Like a pale, sweet echo, morning broke over the holding. A single blossom caught in Jennet's braid. Breathing in with delight, she savored the moment and laughed, charmed, as a marani butterfly—like a lailiki petal come to life—settled on a branch.

Aedan stirred, felt that touch of laughter like a caress. He could feel the soft lailiki blossoms, their fragrance filling his chamber. Wreathed in contentment, he loosed his hold on sleep and came out of bed as wide awake as the holding cat. Dowsing cold water on his face, he dressed in shirt and trousers and padded downstairs, letting himself out, his feet unerring on the water path.

Images of Jennet's progress surrounded him. At some point his breath caught, and he smiled at that shared start in Jennet's breath, was aware when she turned from the river meadows and hurried along the path. Toward him. Sunlight made a nimbus about her blonde head, sparkled in the dancing iris of her eyes. A breeze riffled Aedan's dark, shining curls, warmed the bronzed features, the searching gaze that caught her with a grin on her mobile, curving lips.

Face to face they stood upon the path. Aedan put out his hand. Jennet spread her fingers taut against his own. His curled to grasp hers, and if any had been watching, they would have sworn it was only some trick of movement and shadow that it made it seem as if those hands melded into one. But all else slept in that cool morning; no one stirred and only the rippling of the Settern's placid surface reflected two lovers meeting on the water path, like another pair of lovers long ago.

Like Mikal and Anja, Jennet thought. Or was it Aedan's thought that sounded in her mind? No matter. Here was heart's ease and peace, the Sindren contagion pushed back from hill and valley, town and village. The Five Crowns of Aranth paid no tribute to Mamut, and time was theirs for the stealing this morning.

As the soft light faded about their hands, Jennet sighed with pure happiness, stretched like the holding cat, and locked her hands behind Aedan's neck, his coming around her waist. Then the dark head bent to the blonde and a wordless, glowing vow passed between them, witnessed by the river and the light.

www.ingramcontent.com/pod-product-compliance
Lightning Source LLC
Chambersburg PA
CBHW032246310726
48973CB00008B/2317